# I Spy a Scarecrow

By Bradon Nave

Beacon Publishing Group
ISBN (Paperback): 978-1-961504-22-6
ISBN (Hardcover): 978-1-961504-23-3

I Spy a Scarecrow
© 2025 Bradon Nave

Cover Layout by Lori Pace
Edited by Gerard Hernandez



Beacon Publishing Group, New York, NY 10001
www.beaconpublishinggroup.com

Manufactured in the United States of America

# Dedication

*For my family*

# Table of Contents

# Part I: Drake

# Chapter One

"Good night, moon. Good night, stars. Good night old, broke-down cars…fuck you, Quebec."

Nothing against my northern neighbors. It was my lapse in judgment—maybe hers? Who knows?

The atmosphere is opaque with the songs of countless crickets and toads—other unlovable things of the nightly hour. I loved her. She was a nightly creature, but I loved her. *Loved.*

There's something off about tonight. Some strange element to the evening that keeps reeling me back to *her*.

A coyote's cry impales the serenity, eerie with a lowly quality…yet soothing as I listen from my front porch with a cold beer in hand. Seconds later, the night is teeming with the calls of what must be dozens of coyotes. Their ravenous quest is officially underway. I shouldn't admire them. My clientele expects me to despise coyotes for the havoc they wreak on local livestock. Cruel and heartless, disease-ridden devils. Or perhaps, cunning and resourceful…and devoted parents.

Either way, they're welcomed to feast heavily on the plethora of jackrabbits in the open fields around our home.

*Our home.* Eva, Oklahoma. I don't reside in an actual town, or even the remnants or makings of a town. Eva's the scattered components of a community. Country homes speckle county roads for miles and miles. Flat plains as far as the eye can see. Between these homes, dappled along long stretches of highways, are foul-smelling pig farms. Sets of industrial barns can be seen all about the area. The barns come in groups of five and host Olympic-swimming-pool-sized vats of swine sewage next to them. Each farm is but a few miles from the next, so the area is perfumed with pig shit on any given day. I don't care, I'm used to it, and the pigs are what initially brought us here.

The only scent in the air tonight is an oncoming rain. Or…perhaps the sky will only tease at the idea of downpour as it frequently does—leaving the area parched and praying. Some go so far as to post plywood signs begging passersby to pray along with them. Pray for rain. I'm parched too. *Certainly, drinking with the barn cat doesn't count as drinking alone?*

I'm warm, feeling philosophical, and wishing I had someone to converse with. Not that waking my five-year-old daughter to keep me company on a Saturday night would ever be an option, but I'm lonely, so the thought momentarily crosses my mind.

Standing, stretching, my journey indoors for beer is

abruptly halted as my gaze settles on the cat. His honey-glazed eyes are two perfect capital O's. Back arched, he stares into the dark as if it's conspiring to swallow him whole. He's thicker now—each hair of his worn coat is erect as he growls and grumbles a warning to some invisible intruder.

"What the hell is wrong with you?" My question is ignored. The pale light above frames my shadow on the worn wood below, stock-still, other than my head as I glance repeatedly from my pet to an Oklahoma infinity—spotted with stars and humming with nightlife.

Be it alcohol or ignorance, I'm descending the porch steps. "You coming?" I look back to see the gray flash of a scurrying cat as he disappears around the side of the wraparound porch. Thoughts of lurking barn owls perched in oak trees, or even an ambitious coyote, have me kicking at the ground and trotting confidently toward the barn.

I'm surrounded by vastness. The night's symphony has paused at my disruption as if I've just burst through the door of choir practice.

It happens sometimes while walking to the car in a dimly lit parking lot. Or while working outside in the evening and the shadows hide just enough to evoke more than imagination. Perhaps it's a self-preservation mechanism that every human is blessed with. My feet tingle, as if they're wet. Each little hair on the back of my neck stands at attention. My gaze remains affixed to the openness before me but everything in my being tells me to turn and run—get the fuck out of here…now!

The night can keep whatever it's hiding. I walk

briskly to the porch. The atmosphere is comfortably warm, yet the event leaves my forearms dotted with goosebumps.

Like a child playing tag, I scramble up the steps of the porch as if it's my safety, and peer out once more. "Chill out, dude. Field mice and jackrabbits," I mutter.

Nerves settled, I grab a beer from the fridge and return to my chair, convinced I'm being silly and possibly dramatic.

I have a stack of 'to-be-read' books on my nightstand. A good book could go nicely with chilled beer.

The hum of a distant rig engine is overcome by some vehicle. Headlights appear, and I smirk as a blue Accord comes into view, sending dust up and into the low dim of the porch lights as it comes to a stop and the engine dies.

"Ashlyn?"

Exiting her vehicle, she offers a sly smile. "Hello, man who never answers his calls…or texts."

"*Never*? So definitive. It's Saturday. Phone's on the nightstand."

Ashlyn makes her way up the steps. Her straight brown hair comes just past her shoulders and complements her dark brown eyes and freckled nose. She's typically make-up free and dressed casually. She's genuine, kind, and present, everything Renee was not.

"You got another one of those?" Her tone's off. Her day must have been a colorful one.

Motioning her in my direction, I watch her cautiously peer through the screen door.

"Coty's upstairs, sleeping," I say softly, tugging at

the hem of her shorts.

She sits on my leg, kissing my cheek. "You really don't have your phone?"

"Huh?"

Her hands gently prod at my front pockets before resting on my belly.

"It's on my nightstand."

"For four hours? If you don't want me coming around—"

She relaxes as I pull her into me, kissing her soft cheek…neck. "Stop that. I promise I left it on my nightstand for movie night with Coty. We watched *Trolls* again. I wouldn't lie to you, Ash."

"'Kay."

"You still want that beer?"

"I wanna sit here a second. You're comfortable."

A scent of vanilla and roses enters my nostrils as loose strands of her hair tickle my neck. Much like the tension in the skies above us, something churns here…something uneasy and initially unidentifiable. *Will it pass or pour down?* "You're all I'd ever want coming around. Believe that, okay?"

"Okay." She smirks, rolling her eyes. "I'll take that beer now."

In the kitchen, she remains guarded. I'm realizing the storm is inevitable. Some storms bring new life, others wash out foundations.

"You're tense. Relax." My hands on either shoulder, I playfully pull her to me. "What is it?"

The hardwoods creak below us. The two-story country home is well preserved, yet nearly one hundred years old.

Her hesitation conjures immense concern. "Ashlyn,

what is it? Talk to me."

Light dances in the darks of her eyes as she smiles beautifully. Her smile's lying; it's sad.

"I don't know where your head's at, Drake."

Instantly, my hands are touching about my face, knocking my ball cap to the floor as I examine my messy-haired head. "It's here. It's right here."

"Dumbass," she replies playfully.

"What's that? What do you mean?" Goofy antics aren't going to get me past this one. I rest against the countertop behind me, hopeful there's kiss at the end of this.

"In a year from now I'd kind of like to have an idea of where I might be, ya know? And I can't do that, and it's because of you. And that, well, it pisses me off." She's not smiling now. Her words and tone aren't the harshest she's used with me, but they have me searching my brain for methods of resolution.

"Ash…Ashlyn. I'm trying. It's been a big adjustment and I'm trying."

"I'm not asking for a proposal, Drake. But goddammit, she's been gone for two years and we've been doing…*this* for nearly a year."

*She*—Renee, my ex-wife. There's no framed memories. Her things have been boxed and stored. Only a few pictures remain in Coty's room, and the rest are tucked away in dark places.

Exhaling forcefully, I find the conversation shocking, yet I'm not shocked. I knew this was coming eventually. "I get it, Ash."

"No, Drake, you don't. Take me on a date. Invite me into your room. Stay the night with me after you have sex with me."

My laughter has her eyes widening. "A date? Where, Ashlyn would this date occur? Pizza in Elkhart? Maybe do some fishing at the Grasslands? Where would I take you on a fancy date?"

"You really are delusional. All I need is a decent bottle of wine, some cheap eats and a blanket under the stars. We've got a piece of Heaven just outside."

"Huh? I wouldn't call the panhandle of Oklahoma, *Heaven*."

"Yeah? Well, maybe you're seeing things wrong. I think I have been too."

Her hand reaches for her keys as my words come leaping from my mouth. "Shit. Wait, no. Don't. I'm sorry, I'm stupid. Don't do this. Don't break up with me like this."

She chuckles as her arms cross defensively. "Break up with you? Fuck you, dude. I had no clue we were even dating. Let your next tag-a-long know. Might make her feel extra special."

Maneuvering past me for the door, it's as if I'm only now seeing how absolutely perfect she is. Perfect for me, and how perfect we are together. But I just sat her aside and beckoned her at my convenience while I sorted my shit. There's no room for dignity in situations like these. Her mind is made up, and it's going to take more than mediocracy to convince her.

"Ashlyn, don't go!" The crack in my voice halts her. She turns, sporting an irritated look. "Please. You're right. I'm sorry. I thought we were okay…and were like, headed in the right direction." Neither eloquent nor poised, my proclamation sounds as pathetic as I must look. "You have no idea how much you mean to me."

"No…I don't." The tears in her eyes ensure she's not only hurt, but she's been hurting a while. Yes, fuck Quebec. Fuck Renee for returning there and abandoning her family, and fuck me for allowing the totality of the circumstances to hurt this beautiful person in front of me.

Just as she turns to leave, I forgo chipping at my walls and completely annihilate them. "Stay the night with me…in my room. In my bed. Talk this out with me. Pl…please. I don't wanna lose you. I can't…I can't lose you, Ashlyn."

My heart's not racing, it's pulverizing itself on my sternum from the inside as Ashlyn turns to me. And then, a thing of beauty. A smile. Small, but the makings of a truce are rarely blatant.

"Your bed? You're not messing with me?" She steps to me.

"My bed." My throat's tight and aches as if a fist is inside, squeezing my trachea.

"Things would have to change, Drake." Her tone is softer, yet her stone-cold composure ensures me the bullet hasn't been officially dodged.

"Tell me, Ash. I'll do it. I mean it."

And then she's chuckling, biting her index finger as her keys dangle from her hand.

"What? What is it?" My frantic question has her giggling harder.

"You. You're a hot mess right now. I had no idea."

"What? No idea what, Ashlyn?"

"I had no idea you'd give a shit if I walked out of that door forever."

"What?" Shaking my head, I walk to her. "Are you insane?"

"No…I'm not. But I nearly drove myself insane thinking the worst when you didn't tell me otherwise. You can't go through life not telling the people you love and care about how you feel. Not all of them are going to give you the luxury of a warning."

Swallowing hard, I merely shrug in defeat. "Okay."

"Come here." Her small hands work their way around my waist, pulling me into her. Her embrace is always soothing and welcoming, but tonight it's something different. Tonight, it comes with a reprieve and a genuine lesson learned.

"I'm sorry. I'm so sorry. I'd never want to hurt you, Ash."

"Shhh." She sways with me silently in the dimly lit kitchen to music, playing only in her mind. Her cheek lies flat to my chest as we cradle one another. Catching our reflection in the window, my gaze falls upon my own second chance—in the making. *Don't mess this up, dude.*

The bedroom is anything but special. Just off the living room on the main floor, it houses my bed, dresser, and a few memories I'd like to give back. For whatever reason, of all the places, this has always felt like Renee's. Even after papers were signed and the daily phone calls with Coty dwindled to weekly…biweekly, and sometimes monthly, it's as if I'm betraying her. No more. This is *my* room. In it, I will do what I wish and invite whomever I please.

"And if Coty comes down here tonight?" She's clearly feeling the situation out…feeling me out.

"There's a lock."

"She can only knock so long before—"

"She never comes down here at night, Ash. And

even so…tomorrow starts a different day."

"Oh?" Her bra slides from her arms and to the floor.

From the bed, I nod. "I'm telling Coty tomorrow. And then…and then I'd like to plan something…like a mutual meeting place—"

"You're being serious right now?"

"Yeah. Is that okay?"

The uncontrollable grin etching across her face assures me it is. "A bit one-eighty-ish, but totally cool."

"I meant it, Ash."

"I know that now."

The last shred of remaining guilt seems to have impacted my ability to undress at lightning quick speed at any mention of potential fornication. She glances at my underwear; her smirk of disapproval assures me she has other ideas. Within seconds I've wriggled free of my boxers. Twirling them on my index finger, I send them sailing toward her.

"Daddy?" Her tiny voice halts me mid-thrust.

I look to Ashlyn as our goals are rapidly modified. No longer chasing the *big bang*, pupils bouncing about for something to pop out and make sense. *Escape, hide…what?*

"Coming."

Reaching for my jeans, I zip them up carefully and creep to the door…letting myself out and closing it behind me.

"Hey, Coty."

Eyes barely pried, stuffed Poppy-Troll in arm, my sleepyhead takes my hand and tugs me in the direction of the staircase.

Upstairs, our hands still clasped, she yawns petitely. "Tell…tell me again. Say it again, Daddy." Her eyelids flutter as I bring the comforter to her chin.

In a tiny bedroom of a 1920-ish two-story farmhouse, I once again lay my gaze upon the most beautiful scene in the history of histories…my peaceful, healthy, happy daughter, is somewhere between dreams and reality.

"Now's the time to close your eyes, chase your dreams like fireflies. Perhaps tonight, you'll sail the seas, or play patty cake with chimpanzees. A pirate? A princess or even maybe, the caretaker of dragon babies. Some are silly, some are sad. Dreams are dreams, good or bad. But rest assured, some come true. Come morning light I'll still have you." She's out before I even finish our secret saying.

Her light brown hair looks as though she styled it with a mixer just before bed.

Ashlyn's presence from the hallway was made aware well before. The creaky floors of our home make it impossible to move about unnoticed, even for agile long-distance runners.

In the hall, Ashlyn quietly leads the way down the stairs to the living room and to the kitchen.

"Dragon babies. I love that part." She opens the refrigerator and grabs a beer.

"Yeah…they're not born huge. Don't you watch *Shrek*?"

"Did you write that little poem?" She grins, biting her bottom lip.

"I did. I write a lot of things."

"So mysterious. Dr. Drake Graves. Veterinarian and masterful poet…and excellent father."

Beaming, I slide her beer from her hand for a sip, reaching under her t-shirt with my free hand. "And a…a wild tiger in the bedroom?"

Her hand slaps over her mouth to saddle her laughter. "A tiger?"

I'm laughing too at this point. "Yeah, a wild one. I couldn't think of anything else to say."

Her arms around my waist, head to my chest, she squeezes me. "Let's go."

"Where?"

Our gazes lock as she leads me toward the bedroom. "We're not done."

# Chapter Two

Sunday mornings are never much more than comfortable attire and casual cleaning.

Looking out the window above the kitchen sink, I set my gaze upon an empty nest—nestled within the clutches of the small, dead apple tree. The robins are gone now. Left behind is all that remains of two ambitious creatures, dedicated to their species' cause. Some might see nothing more than a lice-infested mess of feathers, droppings, and twigs. I see a monument to their success.

I'll chop the dead tree down soon. It's only upright because of the robins and their home. So simple, yet so effective. She'll guess it, though, so I set my sight upon something else.

"I spy, with my little eye…something…something small."

From the couch in the living room, she giggles. "How small, Daddy?"

"Oh…as small as a frog."

"Is it a frog?" There's escalating excitement in her voice as she patters to the kitchen. "Do you see a frog?"

"No. And no cheating. Your rules. Back to the living room."

"Is it…is it…give me a clue."

Her tiny doll, tucked among the dandelions, was recently thought to be a casualty. Coty had spent hours searching for the figurine the week prior. "It's wearing a blue dress."

Again, her feet are slapping on the hardwood. "Huh? Frogs don't…*Sabrina*!"

"You guessed it."

"Where?" Jumping up and down enthusiastically, her excitement is uncontrollable.

"Were you visiting the birds last week?" With this information, Coty races out the kitchen door. I watch as she happily reclaims her three-dollar treasure before bolting back inside.

"Daddy! She's totally okay!" Her grin is infectious as she presents a mildly sun-bleached Sabrina.

"Delightful. Now go wash that syrup from your face."

Happy singing resounds from the living room and fades. I'm once again left with my thoughts. Ashlyn left only two hours before. We'd had a long night…but a *damn* good one. Reminiscing on the good parts, my nostalgia is shattered suddenly.

"Ooohhh, Daddy." Little words carry from the living room.

"Yes…Coty."

"I spy, with my little eye, something big."

"I don't want to play—"

"It's my turn, though."

I sigh, drying my hands as I walk to the coffee pot. "Bigger than…a coffee cup?"

"Lots bigger." Her voice is muffled, as if her face is pressed to the large window behind the couch. The window I just cleaned.

"Is it bigger than Biggles?"

"Yes."

"Okay, but it doesn't count if *it is* Biggles. Is it Biggles?"

"No, Daddy. Silly."

"I give up. Did you wash your face?"

Doll in hand, she returns—she's apparently made something of an effort to clean the syrup from her face, but it's ineffective.

"Coty, you're just going to have to take a—"

"I spy a scarecrow," she says slyly.

*Silly head.* She may have an excellent memory, but we removed that raggedy scarecrow from the field months ago when the winter winds took the remainder of its plaid shirt. It was here when we bought the place and I haven't any crops to protect from thieving crows.

"Hmmm. No, ma'am. I think maybe you're mistaken, brat."

"Am not. And I'm *not* a brat."

"Coty," my tone much sterner, "what have we said about being dishonest?" I lift her to me, making direct eye contact as I take her in my arms.

"I would never lie to you, Daddy. I seen—"

"Saw."

"I saw a scarecrow in the field." Her tone and expression assure me she's convinced of what she's proclaiming.

"Really?" And then my brain produces the only rational explanation…*Jakabie Mathews*. I carry her to the window to look upon nothing but our old barn, an open field, scattered clouds and a sleeping Biggles, the haggard barn cat. I then glance upon my daughter's look of bewilderment.

"Daddy…he was out there. I promise."

"I believe you, sweetie."

"Where could he have gone?" She continues peering through the glass from my arms.

"Maybe your scarecrow was actually Jakabie?"

"*You think?* Can I go see? Can we play?"

We head in the direction of the main floor bathroom. The claw foot tub is huge and perfect for childhood antics. "Nah, Coty. Today I'm going to introduce you to a very special friend of mine."

And instantly she's shrieking with delight. "Oh, Daddy! A horse? Or, let me guess, a pig?"

Chuckling as I set her down in the bathroom, I shake my head. "No, Coty. I'm not taking you to work with me. This friend is human…a person."

"Oh." She stares curiously.

"A girl or…woman person," I say with a certain amount of hesitation.

Two seconds of awkward silence pass. "A girlfriend?"

My face heats as if I'm inches from a campfire. "Um, well, uh…yes, Coty."

She shrugs casually before undressing. "Okay. Can we go to Dairy Kream today? I want a cherry vanilla Coke."

Relief is instant. "Whatever you want, baby-dork."

"That's right, Daddy-dork."

***

Dairy Kream isn't a rip off of any large fast-food joint. The establishment is nothing more than a blue cinderblock building, tucked away among churches, near the elementary school in the little town of Elkhart. Elkhart is about a twenty-minute drive from my house and nestled next to the community of Eva.

The menu on the Dairy Kream should read, 'Comfort-Food' near the top. It was basically my mainstay when Renee left. Little Bit and I would load up and head in to town at least three times a week for burgers, tots, chili dogs…*the good stuff.*

Initially I believed Elkhart to be nothing more or less than any other tiny town I'd visited. There aren't many options for those passing through. Drivers needing to relieve themselves after nine in the evening would be better served elsewhere.

The people are pleasant enough, but again, nothing initially struck me as outstanding. Pieces of the town appear untouched by time, yet in a good way. The brick buildings and streets have unique character and each time I drive down Main Street I find myself allured by some enchanting small-town store front display coaxing me inside.

Not long after Renee left I learned how boring I was. I had no life. I found myself frequenting small town auctions at the City Hall on Saturdays and Coty and I would sit in the stands during home games to support the local junior high and high school teams.

It wasn't until I was absorbed and welcomed into the crowd I was sitting among that I realized I didn't want to simply pass through. I was home. *This is my home.*

Coty and I had a lengthy discussion regarding what might be appropriate discussion and what was entirely off limits during our date with Ashlyn. Coty's choice of a mutual meeting place is no surprise at it is inclusive of a playground and more than likely other small children, given that it is a weekend.

Cunningham Park sits in the heart of Elkhart and is surrounded by a waist-high stone and cement fence. Charming, and boasting established trees and two log cabins for the Scouts, it's the perfect common area, regardless of the heat outdoors. There's plenty for Coty to do. Rather than swing, play on slides, or monkey bars, she elects to sit at the pavilion, post meals with Ashlyn and me. The two seem to be hitting it off as if they're long lost friends.

Ashlyn has never failed to impress me, but listening to her converse freely with Coty on topics such as LOL Dolls and Purple Pretzel Daycare, I see it's clear that Ashlyn has done her homework.

"Also, Ashlyn, today I thought I spided a scarecrow…but no. It was silly Jakabie playing in the field. I couldn't go play though, because I had to meet you." Coty sips her drink. "That's okay though, because now we're friends."

"Yes. We. Are." Ashlyn looks to me. "Jakabie? He was in the field?"

"He's harmless. He's a great kid."

"I know, but did you call his parents? He shouldn't be in the field alone."

I shrug. "Maybe you're right. He goes running and exploring all the time, but his mother is usually outside gardening."

Producing my phone, I call the Mathews' residence. I'd treated a heifer with mastitis the week prior and the only way to contact them is the landline, as if they are stuck in 1985.

*"Hello?"* a deep, happy voice answers.

"Robert?"

*"No. No sir, this isn't Robert."*

"Jakabie?"

*"Yes sir."*

"Glad to hear you made it home. This is Drake."

*"Oh. Oh, yeah. Hi."*

"Jakabie, if you'd like, I think we're going to make some homemade ice cream this evening. You're more than welcome to join us."

*"Yes. I would. That sounds like the best idea."*

"Okay then. You clear it up with your folks. I'll give you a ring when we get home to work out the details."

*"Okay, sir. I will. Thank you, sir."*

The drive home is as open as the views and lands around us. Coty asks rapid-fire questions and they're answered diligently, as if Ashlyn had been provided a copy of the interrogation prior to the date. *She's seriously perfect.*

Reprieve comes in the form of Taylor Swift as Coty quells the cross-examination and demands the radio is amped up while she sings and dances along from her booster-seat.

As Ashlyn takes my hand, I realize this could be it. This could be my life…my forever life. I'm an idiot for not acting more quickly, but all good things need time to cultivate. *This is cultivation.*

Rather than homemade ice-cream, we opt for a game of tag in the front yard before finding Biggles basking near the barn. He is brought to the porch involuntarily to be brushed and petted relentlessly. Thankfully, the old fella seems to be a good sport about it.

Small talk leads to frequent hugs, and soon enough, Ashlyn is Coty's "best friend," and she's even sitting in her lap. The evening is fast approaching…as is the end of what has been an incredible revelation of a weekend.

From the porch, the three of us bid the day goodbye as the summer sun kisses the sky goodnight, leaving it blushing a brilliant orange, pink, and pale blue in the distance.

"Let's get you to bed, Coty."

"Please…please no." She yawns sleepily from my arms.

"Tomorrow starts a brand new day, baby-girl."

At Coty's insistence, Ashlyn is invited upstairs to partake in our nightly tuck-in ritual. There's nothing intrusive here…there's nothing awkwardly rushed or mildly disingenuous about the interactions. On the contrary, it's as if some blossom of a relationship has been aching to bloom…and I have been keeping it from budding or taking root. It's sprouting beautifully before me now.

"Daddy…I don't wanna go to Ms. Gonzalez's tomorrow. Can I go to work with you?" She squeezes her Poppy doll—snug from her comforter.

"No, Coty. I've got a full day tomorrow."

Coty offers no resistance, only a diverted gaze and a serious look of disappointment. And then I'm gently nudged from behind.

"Let me stay here with her tomorrow." I'm surprised Ashlyn's excited whisper isn't overheard.

"You don't work?"

"No…not until Tuesday." She grins excitedly. *This is something she genuinely wants to do.*

"Okay, but that means you're staying the night again." I smirk, my index finger dips into her bellybutton beneath her thin t-shirt.

"Deal."

After several seconds of jumping on the bed and announcing a hastily prepared, impromptu agenda for the following day, Coty is calmed and corralled and once again tucked in. The news of her day together with Ashlyn will undoubtedly have her awake with excitement for a bit longer.

"Say it! Say it, Daddy!"

I sigh, smiling, knowing Ashlyn has heard our silly poem prior to tonight…but knowing I must recite it directly in front of her has me bashful for some reason. *It's all for the sake of Coty, I guess.* "Now's the time to close your eyes, chase your dreams like fireflies. Perhaps tonight—

My words are abruptly interrupted by thunderous knocking on the front door. I instantly imagine whomever is on the other side to have some catastrophic emergency requiring immediate veterinarian assistance. It's happened before, multiple times…yet never quite this late.

"I'll see who it is." As I rise from my daughter's bed, she appears more irritated than concerned. Her nose crinkles as though she's smelled something bad.

"Daddy…you'll come back and read me a story?"

"Not tonight, Coty."

"You'll finish our saying?"

"Yes…Coty, later."

Down the stairs and across the living room, I'm growing irritated as the knocking has continued without rest—a steady hammering, shaking pictures on the walls near the front door. I open it to see a wild-eyed Jakabie.

He merely grins and walks past me as I stare in disbelief.

Ruffled and glancing about, the eighteen-year-old meanders into the kitchen.

"Jakabie," I follow him. "Hey bud, what are you doing?"

Happily seating himself at the small kitchen bistro, he looks to me. "I…well. I waited for you to call or come by. You never even called me, sir. You just left me sitting there. You never came for me and you didn't call. So I just came. I'll take vanilla, please." His gleeful grin has me squirming in guilt.

"Oh. Yeah." Frantically searching the freezer, I'm thankful to find vanilla ice cream. It isn't homemade, but I can doctor it up.

I watch him devour his chocolate-syrup covered treat. Looking at him, one might not assume at first glance that he's nothing more than a curious, *special* kid. He chops wood and tends to chores at his parents' farm and I rarely see him absent a smile. Jakabie's masterful intellect is deliberately disregarded by so many, simply because of how he processes.

"Okay, bud. So, I'm assuming you walked here?"

He shakes his head. "No."

"Did your parents drop you off here?" I'm put off at the thought of this as it's nearly nine in the evening.

"No, they don't know. I left out the front door again after they went to bed. I didn't walk…I ran all the way. The entire time."

"Jakabie, you promised your parents you wouldn't leave like this anymore. They took the nails out of your window frames so you can open them at night and listen to the crickets…you've broken their trust now. You can't go running down dirt roads at night and playing in fields—"

"You. You told me. You told me, though. And you wouldn't lie to me. You didn't call. I came here when you didn't call and made sure." With that, he takes his last bite.

"Made sure what, Jakabie?"

"I made sure. I made sure you made it home safe. You didn't call. You wouldn't lie to me."

His words are the words of something completely innocent, purer than innocent…innocence with conviction and heart-felt interest for those he cares about.

I look him square in the eye…and lie. "I was just about to call you right before I heard you knocking on the door, bud. I'm sorry."

Lies are always putrid, but this one has him smiling.

"I need to get you home, Jakabie."

"Okay. Are you mad at me?"

"No, bud. I'm not mad at you."

With Ashlyn's well-founded concerns put to rest, I load Jakabie into my vehicle and head to the Mathews' residence about a mile down the dirt road. He's happy, looking out over the vast flat nothing, up at the endless sky.

"Jakabie, you're very special to me…you know that."

"I'm. I'm. You're special. I love you. I love you and Coty."

I look to the appreciative, intelligent, and kind-hearted young man in my passenger seat. "Love you too, Jakabie." Out of complete stupidity, I forget the golden rule. In a gesture of friendship, I lightly rest my hand on his shoulder.

"No! No, no. Please. Don't touch!"

"Oh! Shit. I'm sorry, Jak. My bad, bud. I totally forgot."

The startling incident has my hands at ten and two on the wheel. Jakabie's gaze settles to the floor in what appears to be guilt.

"Hey, Jakabie. No worries. That was totally my fault. We cool?"

"Yes. Yes. We're okay. Cool. We're cool."

The Mathews' farm is quaint, yet well kept. The land has been in their family for generations. Walking to the front door of the stucco home, Jakabie appears uneasy. The area is dark, nothing stirs but the insects buzzing about the porchlight.

"I won't. I won't be. I…" He inhales deeply and appears to be overly upset. "Now I won't be able to see you for a while." Head down, his posture slumped in a defeated manner, Jakabie extends his index finger— preparing to press his own doorbell.

"Wait, Jakabie." Against my better judgment, I prepare my offer.

"You promise me you won't go off traipsing through fields and down these roads at this hour…and we'll keep this our secret. Just sneak back inside."

"Really?" His eyes widen, as does his smile. In his excitement he hugs himself, a full embrace.

"Really." I chuckle. "Go, bud, before you get us both caught."

He disappears into the house as I make my way back to the truck and back to my own home.

Jakabie had the right idea. Ashlyn and I share a bowl of vanilla in the kitchen before we prepare for bed.

"He really is extremely intelligent. Sometimes I feel like they've tried so long to unlock this…potential. The reality is, there isn't anything that needs unlocking. He simply needs the right tools. There's nothing broken about him." I look up to see Ashlyn's gaze heavy upon me—a whimsical look slapped across her face.

"You, Drake Graves, are a beautiful man."

Smirking, I belch loudly. "How's that for beauty?"

"Nice effort."

"I wasn't even trying."

She grins. "Let that settle. I'll make us some chamomile tea."

I lean forward. "You ready for tomorrow?"

She nods. "I have been for a while now."

Reminiscing on the day, I look to her. "I feel I've taken my time, ya know?"

Giggling, she merely smirks.

"Like, time just goes. We can tally it and track it to make it make sense, but then a year just goes by without…without…" I look to my hands. "I love you, Ashlyn."

As our gazes meet, I see her eyes glisten. She swallows hard, pushing her hair behind her ear.

"I mean that. I haven't said it, and I should have. I only have the future and I know…all I know is I want a future with you, and Coty. I want today, every day."

Tears stream as her lips mouth an inaudible, *I love you too.*

# Chapter Three

My work life includes a great deal of guessing. I often guess what my schedule will look like. Most days I guess why the hell I even bother with a schedule. I'm thankful to have understanding clients. Perhaps they're more needing than understanding. I also guess what emergent situations might take me from the clinic and to the field, and therefore I guess what time I will ultimately be home.

Glancing at case notes on the kitchen counter just before departing, a sense of fulfillment has me uplifted. It isn't the coffee, I haven't had any. It's the three of us under one roof.

"Sleep okay, boyfriend?" Ashlyn sips her coffee from the bistro. My tattered t-shirt has never looked more appealing than it does now on her.

"Um…surprisingly well. I don't think I woke up once."

She chuckles, giving a wink. "Must have been the company. What time does Little Bit usually wake up?"

"She'll come down around nine or so, looking for cereal and strawberries."

"Sounds amazing."

A goodbye kiss, *the goodbye kiss,* and I'm off. Kissing Ashlyn on my front porch, leaving her and Coty to spend the day together…is this our new normal?

The morning air is heavy. The skies didn't tease last night, they poured down. Drawing a breath feels unnatural and requires effort under the humidity of the already sweltering morning sun. *It's only seven.* The lawn is speckled in drops of dew reflecting the morning's rays like thousands of tiny eyes staring up at me as I climb into my truck.

Other than pig farms and telephone lines, homesteads speckle the flatlands. Established farm houses in the country are typically easy to identify, as many of them come surrounded by some of the only trees around for miles. If I were in the business of burglary, I'd simply look for the collections of trees on the prairie.

Twenty minutes of drive time and I'm here. My practice is growing, but isn't quite the respected establishment it will be in a few years' time. Still, progression is obvious. I now have the assistance of Delphine. Her smile basically oozes from the earpiece when I hear her on the opposing end of the phone line. When she's not manning the phones, taking appointments, and keeping my head attached, the nineteen-year-old future veterinary tech student assists me tableside with minor procedures and keeps my practice running smoothly. From Monday through Friday, I can count on her assistance from nine-thirty in the morning to five-thirty in the evening. The building I rent was vacant for years and sits just outside of Elkhart on the highway.

My specialty is anything with hooves. Horses, bovines, and swine…the occasional goat or sheep is sometimes housed or seen at my facility. However, the size and nature of my clients mean that much of my work is done away from the office. It's easier to bring a bag to a horse than a horse to a bag. Emergency operations are another matter.

Renee and I moved here from Boston after I finished school. I accepted a job with the large pig farm as a company veterinarian. My job and marriage disintegrated rapidly, but I fell in love with the slower pace of the area and many of the people. I found it strange initially, to be waved at by complete strangers while driving down the road. That strangeness is something I value now, something I crave. I'm perplexed when passing vehicles and the driver doesn't return my friendly gesture.

There are no hooved things awaiting me as I pull up to my practice, only a frantic-looking woman scrambling from her older Buick at the sight of me approaching. Still wearing her nightly attire, she wobbles to the rear of her vehicle. Fear and mascara streak her face as I park my truck and rush to her.

"Ma'am."

"Help me! It's Jones! Oh, my Jones is in a bad way."

I peer into the tattered Budweiser box housing the agonized cat. It twists and stretches within its confines, completely miserable. "A bad way, indeed." I lift the box and motion the woman toward the door.

"Thank you. This is neighborly of ya."

"My keys…do you mind unlocking for me, Ms…"

"Patricia Lewis."

"Ms. Lewis."

Inside my humble practice, I settle Ms. Lewis in the waiting room and remove Jones from the filthy blanket beneath her in the examining room. It isn't often I'm treated with feline patients. After situating the cat in a comfortable crate, I make my way down the wood-paneled hall to ensure Ms. Lewis hasn't succumbed to a nervous breakdown.

"Please, just stay calm. I've examined Jones and anticipate at least six or seven kittens—"

*"Kittens?"* A hefty arm rests upon a hefty hip. "What the hell did you just say to me?"

Taken aback, I repeat the guestimation.

She slaps her thigh, chuckling uncontrollably. "You's about a piss ignorant fool if you think I'm fallin' for that. Dumb bastard. Jones don't got nuts, but his pecker's there just the same as yours." She points to my crotch, a shade of red cascading over her plump face.

"Ma'am, please, come with me."

She isn't red long, almost white rather, as fifteen minutes later she witnesses the first wriggling, slimy grand-kitty enter the world. The series of insults and crass *pecker* comments continued up until this moment. Now she stands silenced while Mr. Jones cleans her first baby, eating placenta and umbilical cord as if it's a treat.

"You see, Ms. Lewis. Perhaps I'm not as ignorant as you'd originally believed?"

"H...how?" She steps to the crate, peering in, in complete bewilderment.

"I'm assuming you're somewhat versed in reproduction?"

She nudges me in the ribs. "No, dipshit, I mean, how the hell did I not know my baby-boy was a baby-girl…and a little whore at that."

I chuckle. "It happens more often than you might think."

Ms. Lewis looks to be at least sixty and somewhat scattered in nature. "Is Jones your only cat?"

Rolling her eyes as she looks to me, she sputters back, "Well, obviously not now."

"Prior…to this."

"Yeah," she replies.

"You'll be fine. She's doing great, and after the kittens are weaned, we can spay her so—"

"I can't afford none of this. Do I look like I can afford this shit?"

I'm unsure whether to find her offensive or humorous, but regardless, she is undeniably entertaining. "I'll make you a deal. You promise to bring the kittens back for their vaccinations…and possibly refrain from calling me ignorant," I grin slyly, "and we'll call it even. I'll help you find the little ones good homes, too."

She looks at me as though I'm being ridiculous. "Deal."

Patricia left with her brood just after the last of the five kittens was born, and now I'm cleaning up and preparing for the remainder of my day…wondering how I might catch up without cutting corners. I'm thankful to hear the slamming of a car door. Delphine.

Easily the most collected young adult I've acquainted myself with, Delphine is never late. Her departure for school in a few weeks is something I need to take into consideration as it's clearly going to impact my ability to operate effectively.

"Hello, Drake." She enters with a smile and immediately heads for the computer system.

"Good morning, Delphine. Let me guess. I'm behind?"

She grins. "Um…why are you still here? You're booked solid today."

"It was a kitten emergency."

She scratches her blonde hair and seats herself. "Okay. I'm going to make some calls. We'll need to push some stuff back until…can you squeeze anything in past five on Wednesday?"

My vibrating pocket goes ignored as I skim my planner. The caller immediately attempts again. I look to my screen to see Ashlyn's name.

"Hello there—"

*"She's not fucking here!"* Her shrieking words don't initially penetrate. I only know that something is wrong.

"What? Ashlyn?"

*"Coty is gone! She didn't come down! She's not in her room!"*

My mind scrambles. Her words are senseless. I understand them, yet it's like I'm listening to them from the TV or radio.

*"Drake!"*

"Ashlyn…you're sure? You've looked…you've looked under her bed and—"

*"Yes!"*

"Oh my god. Shit. Call the police. I'm coming home."

Delphine stands, walking to the door as I'm opening it. "What…what's going on, Drake?"

"Clear my appointments today, Delphine. I'll call you in bit."

I'm driving under water, or possibly in someone's nightmare. This foggy cruelty isn't my life, it can't be. Waiting to emerge or awaken, I tear down the old highway toward my house without looking at the speedometer even once. There isn't time to cry, react, or respond to anything. I only know my heart is racing, pounding violently through my fingers, eyes, and ears.

My truck slides to a halt in my drive. My hopes that this is all a dramatic misunderstanding are shattered as Ashlyn appears belligerently on the porch.

We collide mid-steps and crash on them in each other's embrace. It's only now I realize this cruelty is indeed reality, and it is mine. "Search! Search the house, the barn—"

"I have, Drake!"

"Tear them down! Turn them over! She didn't disappear! Little girls don't just evaporate! She's here, Ashlyn! She has to be here."

My misery echoes off the tin barn. My cries for my daughter spread out over the yard and then die in the fields surrounding my home. I tear across the farmyard, screaming out her name until it's mush in my mind. Over and over until there's nothing more than a squeaking cackling of what was my voice.

The house is in shambles, as am I. I've searched and re-searched every room. My mind teeters on the wrong side of sanity as I look from the living room window to finally see a single squad car come into view.

Casual in his approach, the officer lacks urgency and anything else necessary to find Coty. He scans the premises as he exits the car. Resting his folded arms on his massive gut momentarily, he squints the way confused people do when they hear a word that's evaded their vocabulary. Glancing about my property, he remains beside his car.

It isn't rage or anger even, but the horrifying idea of Coty being somewhere other than close by has me charging out the front door, down the stairs, and toward the now concerned, and wide-eyed, bald officer. I'm but three feet from him by the time I realize he's talking. Mustard stains the right corner of his lips and his ginger mustache boasts crumbs of some baked morsel.

"I said stand down!" he shouts at me. He watches me, frightened, as if I'm some pit bull charging at him.

"Officer." My breath…the crunching rocks beneath my feet. *They're real*. I hear them and they're painfully real. "I need help."

In the kitchen, I pace. My heart is sinking. Penned words may be a necessity, but how can preparing this report not be wasting time? There must be some simple solution. *She's here!* She must be here. I've done everything but rip up the hardwood, and I'd do that with my bare hands at this point if I thought for a second it'd produce my daughter.

Ashlyn's lips quiver in between questions. Her eyes are swollen nearly shut, yet they showcase a lost gaze. I should comfort her. I should cradle her, but I can't think. How can I help Ashlyn when I feel like I can't even *fucking breathe?*

"This was your first day sitting for DeCota?" The portly officer, Nathan Tropes, glances up from his chicken scratch, cocking his head and looking curiously at Ashlyn.

"Yes. It was supposed to be."

"I see." He's writing again.

"You see what?" I snap from near the sink, catching his immediate attention. "What the hell do you see?"

Slow tics of the antique clock on the wall fill the otherwise silent house. *It's too quiet.* She should be singing, laughing…the three of us glance upon each other awkwardly a moment more.

"Ashlyn." The officer drags his thumb across his tongue slowly while reviewing his notes. "Did something happen this morning? Was there say, an argument?"

She looks to me, dumbfounded, and then back to the cop. "An argument? With Coty? No. I told you she never came downstairs. It wasn't until I went to wake her that I realized she was gone."

"So…nothing out of the ordinary?" His pupils slide to the corner of his eyes—aiming at Ashlyn.

"Are you fucking stupid?" Her expression hardens—cements. "She's missing. That's as out of the ordinary as it gets."

"Calm yourself, little lady." He licks his thumb again. *On the Road Again* is hummed softly as he taps his pen.

Pen tapping. Clock ticking…but still no laughter, no singing. Only madness floods my brain and home. "Enough! She isn't missing, you stupid jackass! Get up! She's out there!" I point in the direction of the kitchen window. "She's only gone until we find her, we just need help doing that. So, stop licking your lips excessively and stand up."

I allow him several seconds to absorb my words. When he does, he finally stands, using the wall for support—grubby fingers cling to the aged wallpaper until he's entirely upright and apparently offended.

I can't. Stagnancy makes for the best breeding pools for mosquitos, ill-thoughts, and other life-sucking bullshit. I have to mobilize. I'll run for a mile in one direction until I find her…and if I don't, I'll run for a mile in another. I'll run until she's in my sight or I'm free of this absurdity. She's here. She has to be here.

The screened door slams behind me. My feet are hammers down the front steps as I reenter August's oppressive oven. The world is especially gigantic now that I've lost what I hold dearest…and I don't know where to start.

Running—indecisively zigzagging as if I'm dodging ghosts on my lawn, my gaze rests upon a possible destination…possible answers—*the Mathews' farm*.

Her being there doesn't make sense, but her being anywhere other than where I left her doesn't make sense. Illogical scenarios play out in my head. Thoughts of Coty being gently coaxed away from her home somehow, to play innocent games with the lovable autistic neighbor have my lips curling into a hopeful smile.

The field is endless, as if I'm eternally running. The white stucco peeks at me through the large dogwoods. The chain-link surrounding the home is coming into view. It's choked by twisting honeysuckle vines yet I'm close enough now to see the diamond-like pattern in areas not clad with the greenery.

The hum of the archaic swamp cooler in the Mathews' window assures me I could be inches from answers. There's a burning fire in my chest. Reaching the home, my fist rattles the old front door violently with heavy knocks. Speckles of white paint chips make their way to the cracked cement porch like a summer's snow.

Seconds are decades. Small sparrows hop along the dirt drive, oblivious to my plight. *How am I here?*

Anxiety and black coffee tear up my esophagus, leaving me heaving into the bushes from my mouth and nostrils.

"Hello!" My hand on the rusted doorknob, I turn it, completely expecting it to be locked. The Mathews should be up and tending to gardens or out in the fields at this hour—not indoors. I know that, but for some reason I'm only now taking it into consideration. The knob turns. I push, and to my surprise, the door opens.

The hint of something sinister enters my nostrils. Smoke.

"Hello?" Entering the immaculate home, my gaze sets upon the free-flowing river of white smoke snaking over the popcorn ceiling in the living room. The home is well-lit, yet a faint orange glow beckons me to the dated galley kitchen.

An avocado-green gas range has one burner going. The flames have spread and devoured what appears to be what is left of a roll of paper towels left foolishly in the center of the range.

The kitchen boasts a brown orange carpet with white lines running vertically and horizontally, making squares. Immediately in front of the range, small embers peer up at me from the carpet, as if they're cursing me…knowing I'll soon extinguish their plot to incinerate the atrocious carpet and engulf the home.

With the burner off, the embers stomped and

dowsed, I continue calling. "Hello! Robert! Jakabie!" My aching throat is further compromised by smoke in the air.

There's only memories of the family on the walls and voices coming from a large wood-framed TV set in the living room. "Hello!" Glasses of milk set on the table…and the coffee pot is on.

A small potted cactus sits by the kitchen window. *Arizona, 2016.* Their last vacation, I believe. A red spec catches my attention in the distance out of the same window. There's someone in red walking on the open prairie. They look to be at least a quarter of a mile away and walking toward the cornfield.

"Jakabie!"

I race from the home and toward him. My voice fails me when I try to yell. The spec is getting larger, but before I reach it, it disappears within the stalks.

As I reach the crop line, I look about for the figure and catch my breath. "Jak…Jakabie!" Cracking and raspy, my words rip from my tender throat.

Thick stalks scratch my face as I dart into the corn. The earth beneath me is rows of mounds, and makes it difficult to keep my gaze level and run through the crop.

"Jakabie!" Razors are tearing from my lungs as I call out. Each time I yell is more agonizing than the time before. The insides of my shoes are now filled with soft soil from the field as I continue running aimlessly.

Only now does it sink and settle. *How will I find my way from here?* I'm phoneless and it's all the same from every point of view. Is Coty here, lost in the stalks?

"Coty!"

"Drake?" A gruff, full voice resounds through the corn. "Drake? Is that you?"

The red shirt comes into view, pushes past corn stalks, making his way toward me. The pepper-haired man's haggard skin is colored by years of sun and alcohol. He's tall, thin, and muscular, yet his body seems to ache for mercy…an acquittal from the bottle and the field.

"R—Robert!"

We meet. The heat encompasses us within the thick foliage as the buzzing cicadas sing around us. His eyes, dingy and haunted, ensure me we have something in common this mid-morning. He's also lost what he values most.

"Jakabie? Robert, you can't…you can't find Jakabie?" My words are squeaks and whispers. Sweat invades my eyes.

"No. Tarnation, son, no! How'd you know?" His haggard hands abrasively grip my shoulders, his frantic expression is all too relatable. His gaze begs me for answers I don't have…and yet the sickening taut tension within my gut is easing just enough that I can breathe without the nausea lingering. "Coty. Coty's gone. She's gone, too. They're…it's okay."

"What the heck do you mean, it's okay?"

Turning from him, pressing my thumb and index finger into my eyes, hoping the pressure and black and gold circles will produce something sane, I fall back on my ass in the dirt. "She's with him." Panting still, I look up. "She's okay if she's with him."

Robert looks about, either disgruntled or disordered. "Coty…Coty is gone? When?"

"Today. Now."

"Oh, god." His face now flaccid, I witness something most concerning. Tears etch their way down his creased cheeks. I'd never seen this man smile or even raise his voice. His concern cascades from his eyes and leaves me further sinking in despair.

"Where, Robert, might they have gone?"

Robert turns to me, his head cocked as he offers a sympathetic gaze. "I need to get home, son. I'd suggest you do the same."

"What?" Staggering, I rise to meet him.

"I need…I cast him…" His voice fails him.

"Robert. Where would they be? Here? In the corn?"

He turns from me and solemnly walks away.

"No. Robert. I need…we need to keep looking. They're with each other." I'm on his heels, my gaze locked on the leathery lines in his tanned neck.

"Goddammit, Robert. Fucking look—"

I've heard of the term, 'seeing stars,' but I've never been treated to its etiology. On my back, there's an odd ringing in my ears and muffled words entering them as I realize I've been punched.

"That's the Lord's name, son. Just you head on home, now."

I open my eyes to a brilliant blue sky, framed by the stalks. Blood floods my mouth and nearly chokes me as it pools in the back of my throat. Spitting as I prop myself up and look about the area, there's only a trail of footprints to lead me from this endless scene.

I walk home, my shoes and shirt are soiled and bloodied…my soul eviscerated. I'm thankful to see an additional patrol car as I approach my house. There are no stars, so I wish on clouds, every last one of them. Coty might be there when I get home. There's a chance, a good chance actually. We'll laugh about this at her graduation…I may include something about it to embarrass her in an impromptu toast on her wedding day.

Stationary in the baking heat, I stand in front of the porch steps. Hesitant to relinquish the hope she may be just inside, I remain for a moment more. And then Ashlyn appears.

She races to me, seemingly horrified at my bludgeoned appearance. There isn't the slightest hint of relief in her expression. In this moment, she's prematurely taken my hope. *Thief.* So, in this moment, I'm hating her.

"Oh, my god…oh, my god! Are you okay! What happ—"

"No! No, I'm not fucking okay! My daughter…she's…g—" Too toxic. The words are vile and I'm incapable of saying them. Saying them, admitting it…I can't. I can't be one of *those* parents. How am I the parent of a missing child when only an hour and a half ago I was delivering kittens, contemplating which one I would surprise her with seven weeks from now? Hands to my face, the tears drench my palms. In Ashlyn's embrace, I quickly realize, not only do I not hate her…I wouldn't be standing now if it wasn't for her.

"Mr. Graves?" a female voice calls me from the porch.

Peering from Ashlyn's embrace and through my tears, I look to see a middle-aged officer. She appears sympathetic, seasoned, and most importantly…competent. And this is from a single glance. Her portly colleague is just behind her.

I answer more questions regarding timelines and whereabouts in the kitchen for the new officer, Officer Salizar. More time passes and I'm twisting inside. The further I get from the morning, from our normalcy, the more I feel it slipping away. 'If I'd only,' and, 'if I could just,' should be flooding my mind. Yet, I'm unsure what I did wrong.

There are now four squad cars on our property and one visiting the Mathews' residence. Time should be standing still, but it's sailing by with no regard to my situation.

The language used is indigestible. Seeing officers on my lawn and rummaging through our barn and property has my eyelids on the verge of purging my emotions at any given second.

As the day disintegrates, my anxiety amplifies. The idea that my five-year-old Coty might be out in the fields all night under unknown circumstances is unfathomable.

The officers prepare their lanterns on my lawn while discussing the plan of action. A volunteer search party is to embark across the prairie and fields at dawn should the officers' efforts to find Coty and Jakabie tonight be unsuccessful.

On the porch, Ashlyn and I watch the nauseating scene. The lanterns, the stars, and moon…the fireflies. *Fireflies…shit!* "Dammit." Again, my gaze blurs.

"They'll find them, Drake.

"I know, Ash…but…I lied to her. I promised that I'd…I told her last night that I'd come back and finish our saying. I didn't. What if…if I never see her again? What if she's scared and alone and she knows I lied to her?"

My back slides down the house as my ass hits the porch, hard. Ashlyn is instantly crouched by my side.

"Drake, you'll be tucking her in bed and talking about pirates and dragons and all that fun stuff. I promise. She's not alone."

The one thing, the only thing that is of any comfort to me at this point is that she is with Jakabie. Enraging is the idea that he is the cause of this entire mess. He took her from my home to begin with, but she's not alone. I know he loves her dearly, and when the officers find them tonight, she'll have been kept safe. Jakabie is strong.

The soft thud of Salizar's boots ascending the steps catches my attention. The officer is seemingly hesitant to approach. Her demeanor, the way she carries herself and the way she's conducted herself throughout the afternoon has led me to believe she's seasoned and professional. Now, she lingers several feet back as if she's a child on the verge of tattling on herself. A knot develops in my throat as I stare at her and her gaze continuously diverts from mine. Something's horribly wrong. "What is it?"

"Mr. Graves…Dr. Graves."

"Yes."

She appears to be swallowing stones, staring toward her boots with her hands behind her back. "We've spoken with Robert Mathews."

She produces a large Ziplock baggy as the remainder of my world crumbles.

"What the fuck?" I spring from my seated position, my eyes feeling as though they could bulge from their sockets.

"This was recovered this morning by Robert

Mathews. It was found in the ditch just between your homes."

The big bright eyes of Poppy stare at me from inside the bag. Burgundy blood splatter traces the whites of her eyes and blue dress.

I reach for the bag in disbelief as she withdraws it from my sight.

"I'm sorry. We'll have to send this to the lab…it's evidence now."

"No. No, no, no, no, no." I hug the nearest thing to me, the porch post, and allow it to support the majority of my weight.

"Hey," Salizar snaps. "Stop. This is nothing more than an unanswered question."

"No. That's hers. What else did he…what else did Robert say he found there?"

"Only this."

I've heard people say they're *numb* because of this or that, but only now am I realizing there's a physical numbness associated with shock. *This must be shock.* I watch the lanterns scatter and disperse…absorbed into the evening atmosphere like cinders tossed from a campfire, and I'm left without answers and with troubled thoughts. I can't sit, as my nerves have me wanting to scour the countryside until she's in my arms again. I can't stand as my knees feel wet and weak.

A dizzying nausea leads me to the bistro. My head to the table, and then I'm drifting.

I wake sometime later and am led to my bed. The night comes in visions and scattered fragments. Vivid images are painted on the backs of my eyelids and every sound and voice within my sleeping brain is intense like fever dreams. I hear her. Coty's voice is calling to me from her bedroom up the stairs. My bare feet forcefully slap the groaning steps as I ascend. As I'm nearing the top, the steps extend, and her voice is carried away the length of the flight of stairs. The desperation in her calls intensifies and I'm left to run faster, to sprint. Yet, every time it's the same cruel scenario. I nearly reach the second floor of our home, only to watch the stairs multiply, leaving me to continue the madness.

I catch myself just before her name leaves my lips and wails throughout my room and home. I glance about my room, panting atop my bed, sweating and clenching the sheets. Within the first few seconds of opening my eyes, only two or three seconds, there's room for normalcy. *It's only a dream.* A horrible dream and now it's gone. My wits are quickly regained and I find I'm waking from a nightmare to collide into another. Jumping from the bed, I rush for news of any answers.

Ashlyn is on the porch, staring out into the distance. Weary eyes and laced shoes give the impression she may have been up all night. The instant our gazes connect, I know Coty is still gone. I feel the urge to implode, yet don't. Not today. Today I'll find my baby girl. I can't find her by doing what I did yesterday.

The evening's crusade, I'm told, was fruitless. The investigators roamed the fields and walked the plains before the storms. Now, the volunteers are gathered in vehicles along my lawn and down the drive. They wait patiently for the rain to cease.

Everything is still but the water falling from the sky, and the tiny tributaries running from my yard and down my drive. It's been nearly twenty-four hours. I know only that a loved one has taken my daughter and I'm clueless as to why. Somebody knows something, yet no one is moving. I need to mend myself to the point of obtaining information. *I need to move.*

"Ash. I need you. Can you—"

She walks to me, hugging me. "I've already called my boss. I'm off until we clear this up."

"Thank you."

"I need to run in and grab some clothes. I may rest a while."

"You'll be back tonight?"

"Yes." Her sweet voice is muffled on my chest. "I promised her we'd watch *Purple Pretzel Daycare*. I'm not one to break a promise."

I kiss her cool, dewy cheek before she leaves my arms and the porch for the downpour.

Not long after, her Accord is slipping down the muddy drive and into the soft, rainy gray.

In the kitchen, an exhausted Officer Salizar sits sipping coffee.

"What now?"

"We continue searching. We've covered every inch of three square miles."

"Officer…where would they be? There's nothing here but yucca plants and tumbleweeds and crop fields. They have to be somewhere. They must have gone somewhere."

"We will find them, Drake. Tell me more about Jakabie and Coty's relationship."

Thoughts of hopscotch, puzzles, checkers, and tea parties enter my head. "He loves her. He lets her touch him."

"Excuse me?" She looks up from her notes.

"No. Not…I mean. Jakabie, he's got this thing. No one can touch him, at all. He has some phobia of being touched. But he'll take Coty's hand and sometimes I'd look outside and she'd be kissing his cheek—"

"Would he hurt her, Drake? Do you think Jakabie is capable of hurting Coty?" Her palms lie flat on the table. Her eyes are asking me to consider the question carefully, yet there's no need.

"No. Not at all. I don't know why he took her, but I know he wouldn't hurt her."

"Drake." Salizar's voice is stern, cold. "It's time to get real here. Jakabie is a challenged, eighteen-year-old boy. What could he possibly want with Coty? Why would he have taken her? Can you remember, even once, where you felt uncomfortable leaving them alone together—"

"Jakabie is an intelligent, sweet kid. I let them play for hours, and not because he's challenged, but I know he loves her and I trusted him to keep her occupied."

"You allowed them to be alone for hours unsupervised? How can you say for certain there was no abuse taking place?"

"Abuse?" I envision Salizar's face twisting as my scalding coffee washes over her. I resist.

"It's time to wake up, Dr. Graves. Last night we cradled you. Today you need to check yourself. Your daughter is missing. The only suspect is an eighteen-year-old autistic man, and the only thing we have to go off thus far is a blood-stained doll."

"He didn't hurt her! Do you not hear my words? Maybe…maybe she fell and got a bloody nose."

She chuckles. I suck my lips, my nostrils widen, taking in the coffee stained air as my cheeks twitch in anger.

"Tell me, Drake. This doll—"

"Poppy!"

"Yes, Puppy. How long has she had it?"

"A year. Maybe more."

"And I'm assuming she sleeps with it?"

"Every night. Why?"

"So, after she fell, got this nosebleed…she just left it there…in the ditch, her favorite toy, and she just abandoned it because of a little bloody nose?"

*She's right.* "Fuck you." I stand, making my way from the kitchen and outside.

"Wait. Drake."

Her hand takes my bicep from behind. "No!"

"Help me find her," she says calmly.

I turn to her, my hands pressing either side of my head, squeezing. *"How?"* I shout through clenched teeth.

"Tell me about Jakabie."

"I told you! He loves her. If he hurt her…if he did something…no, he didn't, he wouldn't. I know him."

"Okay. Then tell me. How, Drake, do you know him? Do you know him casually, do you know him—"

"He loves *The Brady Bunch, Happy Days,* and, and basically anything retro. He…likes purple Kool-Aid. When he eats over here, he only wants the crusts cut off three sides of his sandwiches so he can hold it with the one that's left. And he makes me feed the other three to the birds. *See?* Sweet! If I have an issue with my books he can settle it in seconds—"

"Books?"

"My accounts from work…the kid is a genius with numbers."

"You trust him to—"

"Yes! Do you not hear me?" The tension in the air palpable, my throat throbs from the inside out from the previous day's yelling. "You're not dealing with some inbred trailer-park pedophile. This kid is smart and kind. I know him. I *know* him. I trust him in my home, I trust him with my books, and I trust him with my daughter…wherever they are…if she's hurt, we have to find them."

As if something I've said has finally makes sense, her expression relaxes, her arms uncross, and she exhales passively. "Okay."

# Chapter Four

The tub-drain slurps and gurgles, taking my bath water and the previous day's filth away. I tend to my lip in the mirror. The split is slender enough, yet it hurts to make any real facial expression. Not that I would smile or anything, but grimacing hurts—*crying hurts*.

The rains have ceased. I find myself saying "excuse me" repeatedly in my own home. Officers have depleted and replenished my coffee and toilet paper supply.

Minimal effort has gone into drying myself. My t-shirt and shorts are now dampened. Stepping into my sneakers by the door, I walk out of the house without acknowledging the team in my kitchen. Off the porch, I head in the direction of the Mathews' farm. Typically, Biggles will rush to be by my side during morning and evening walks. Today he watches cautiously from the barn side, hesitant to accompany me when I walk by.

I hear someone call me from behind when I get several hundred feet from the house but it doesn't slow my pace. The skies remain gray and my peripheral vision catches movement all around me. The volunteers dance in and out of corn like tiny ants in their dens. So far from me, they are nothing more than dots in the distance.

When I reach the Mathews' home and the front door, I knock politely.

A moment later it budges an inch inward, swollen by the rain, and then it opens. A solitary eye peers at me through the slender opening.

"Robert. Do you have a moment?"

No words, only grunts and sighs as he lets the door fall open when he turns. The doorknob taps the wall inside and I'm allowed to enter. The faint hint of something charred lingers still as I cautiously close the door behind me.

"My apologies." His 's' is elongated. His arms are extended on either side as if he's attempting to maintain stability while walking across a balance-beam. But he's making his way across his clutter-free floor to the floral print couch. *He's seriously hammered right now?*

"For what?"

"Bustin' you in the yapper." He falls back, his head tossed sloppily on his loose neck.

"Yeah. As ridiculous as that was…it's not why I'm here, Robert." I remain standing, looking about the walls and home. Pictures of Jakabie and Maurine are framed and hanging proudly. Other than a few contemporary trinkets and the clothing Jakabie wears in the photos, the home and its innards look preserved from the late 1970's.

"It's a funny thing." His soft statement leaves his mouth between hiccups.

"What? Please, explain to me what you find funny."

Slowly, his face turns. As his staggering gaze locks on mine, one eye is pried wider than the other and his eyelids are drooping, red and saturated in agony and alcohol; he chuckles. "All of it." He continues to hiccup silently. "Life. All ya work for. And then it all irons out and the lucky ones are the ones cryin' because they got nothin' to show for it…then there's me. There's Maurine. We're forever memorialized. Nothin' we done, year after year, will be remembered. Only this. Only what he done. Only what he is."

Staring at the drunken man, it becomes clear he's confident that Jakabie has hurt Coty. "No. No, Robert, we don't know that."

"Ha! You don't know what I know, fool!"

"What?" My pulse pounds. "What do you know? Tell me, please."

He grabs his glass from the stand, chugging the contents, leaving me desperate for information.

"Robert! *Maurine!* Maurine, are you home?"

Again, he's chuckling. "It's…it's about that time." He winks and points in the direction of the master bedroom.

I dash from the living room and through the open door, only to stop immediately. To my horror, Maurine is lifeless atop the queen-sized bed. Her tone is a pale-blue. Initially, I wonder if perhaps the woman's aqua-colored nightgown is casting a shade of cyanosis. As I digest the mayhem…her lifeless pale eyes, pasty, swollen tongue peeking from her blanched lips, it becomes clear Maurine is deceased. It's then my glance settles on the wood paneling near the left of her head. It's painted in what appears to be both blood and brain matter. "What…what have you done, Robert?"

I turn to see him rising. "It was by *her hand!* We answer to one and only one!"

"Robert! Why? Why did she do this? What do you know? Tell me what you know about my daughter."

Stumbling to me, his bottom lip quivering, he places his hand on my shoulder for support. "I know I housed him…I know I fed him. I loved him and I grew him. That makes me responsible. Makes us *just* as accountable. But don't you fret none. There's a special place in his kingdom for young'ns. But there's a special place in the hot spot of hell for monsters and the *fools* who grow 'em up strong!"

"Robert! Please." His gaze, sloppy and pained, remains on me—as does the gaze of a thousand tiny white birds within the wallpaper of the living room. All staring me down, waiting for my reaction and all I can think to do is beg. Plead for his cruel words, the cruelest ever spoken. "Robert…is my daughter…? Did Jak…did Jakabie hurt Coty?"

"Go. It's that time." His expression talks…a horrible phrase. He's sympathetic. I watch twitching eyelids on the brink of spilling tears and a quivering lip, too affected to formulate the words. *Tell me.*

"Robert, please. Tell me."

"What's written on my stone, it won't be factual. What the preacher man speaks up there when they give me back…put me back in the ground. It won't be truthful, neither. I ain't worth the spit flung off his teeth when he goes to spewin' a heap of shit 'bout, 'salt of the earth,' and, 'a righteous man of the Lord.'

He turns his face.

"Robert. You're a good man. You and your wife have always been good people. I know you know something. Don't…please don't do this to me."

"A good man? A good man don't spend his life consumed with what's growin' out in his fields while he's in complete denial of what he's got sproutin' up under his own roof."

"What? No. Robert, I refuse to believe it. I *know* Jakabie." My shoulders back, confident in my proclamation as I witness the crumbling of this stone of a man.

"Oh, I do too, boy. I know him like the back of my good hand. Know my wife, too. She's a strong woman. Never the type what would do somethin' dumb…same bed we loved in for twenty-seven years. I sure know that woman. She'd never do nothin' like puttin' her daddy's pistol upside her melon. Casual as takin' a nap or pourin' sweet tea. You know shit, Drake. We know shit."

"Then what do you know, Robert?"

"I told you. It's time. Get." He turns to me, hand to the wall for support as his head lowers. He cracks further. Soft sobs and some unidentifiable mumbling.

"Robert—"

*"Get out of my house, Graves!"*

I take a step backward. "I can't. I have to know. Why can't you tell me where my baby is?"

He stares at the floor while shaking his head briefly yet rapidly as if he's attempting to get water from his ears. "No."

"Robert." My entirety must be a portrait of desperation.

"My mouth can't say those things. Don't make my last words be those things."

"Those things? Last words? Robert…no…what do

you…"

He stumbles through the doorframe and into the gruesome scene in the bedroom. "You tell Jakabie…you tell that boy when you find him that I was weak. God may forgive…he forgives all. But I ain't God, and that ain't a requirement on my part."

Swallowing hard, I peek around the doorframe to watch Robert climb into the bed with his dead wife. His back to me, I hear him talking softly to her.

"Robert. Robert, I don't think that's a good idea. Come with me…you need help."

"No, boy. You're the one who needs help. For that, I do apologize."

"What?" I step into the room. "Robert—"

"Will you at least try…do me the favor of trying?"

I stare down on the grisly scene—my neighbors cuddled atop blood-soaked bedding. I haven't truly had time to process but it's overwhelmingly clear this requires intervention on a different level. "Try what, Robert?" I dig my phone from my pocket.

He exhales and sighs passively as if he just finished watching the end of a love story. "When you get healed up from this…down the road and years from now, please try to remember me as a decent man, faithful by his wife and right by the Lord."

"Okay, Robert." My gaze bounces from my iPhone to the Mathews in bed as I thumb through my contacts for Officer Salizar.

"I turned my head. But that don't make no damn bit of difference now, try and remember me as a man who grew corn…not monsters. Not a murderer."

"What did you just—" The ringing in my ears isn't initially identifiable. It isn't until I recognize my phone screen's been speckled in a mist of fine red, and the smell of gun smoke hits my nostrils, that I rapidly piece together what has just occurred.

Blood streams from the back of Robert's head, but his hair makes it impossible to identify from where. His body twitches as if he's being mildly electrocuted for a few seconds, and then he's still. I'm still as well—I'm paralyzed in the seconds following.

The noises of the home and my labored breathing gradually overcome the gun's blast. I find myself wondering how their existence was reduced to this, and mine as well.

*He called him a murderer!* And then I realize my daughter is dead. Coty is gone. Since I've known them, the Mathews have been as solid as the church bell across the street from the elementary school in town. Suicide over speculation isn't in their DNA. Whatever knowledge they possessed was so overwhelmingly horrific, they had to escape it—permanently.

As the blood ceases, leaving the pillow just behind his head a brilliant red, I'm left standing in observation of some twisted Romeo and Juliet ending, wrapped in the clutches of hideous secrets. Inhaling the madness, the smells of whiskey-kissed sweat, smoke, and regret…I yell—scream with all I have.

My voice has given out and comes in fragments on my breath, but I'm screaming and I'm unsure why.

The idea of never holding Coty's living hand again has me wondering if taking the gun and painting the wall with my own blood is such a bad idea. I need answers, yet the answers I seek are too merciless. Now, after being served a sliver of information, I stand stunned, knowing those answers were locked within the brains of the two in bed before me. Those brains now cover the bedding, flooring, and wall.

"Drake!"

I turn to the voice behind me. Officer Salizar is the only face I focus on. The rest are faces and blue rushing by me.

# Chapter Five

It smells of grilled cheese and a locker room. Painted cinderblocks surround me. The one-way mirror is just to my right, yet the officers have left the door propped open. Perhaps they don't want me feeling like a perp? I couldn't give a shit less at this point.

The table is long and sturdy. There's good lighting and the chair I'm sitting in is simple yet comfortable. The cop shows I watch on TV showcase a different scenario completely.

A physical ache in my core and chest have my eyelids constantly shuddering as I verge on the point of breakdown. My heart has never been this broken. There's nothing left to piece together.

"Hello?" Salizar enters, closes the door, and sits directly across from me.

"Hi." My hands are firmly clasped.

"Thank you for coming here with me, Dr. Graves. This has just escalated to something more than we'd really anticipated."

I only nod.

"Dr. Graves. We're expanding the ground coverage.

Multiple agencies are involved…I'm hoping to find you answers soon, my friend."

Again, I nod.

"We'll need you to stay clear of the premises—"

"I know. I know about all that. I'm not going home. Not until you tell me I can."

She smiles. It's the kind of lax smile that assures me she's thinking something and she's about to tell me or ask me about it. "What about you, Drake?"

Her voice doesn't echo within our confinements, but it's compact within the room with no place to escape to, so it digs deeper into my ears.

"Huh?"

"How can we help you? You're staying with Ashlyn Ramirez, yes? You shouldn't be driving. You need rest and food."

"I need. I just need to know. That's all I need."

Her forehead creases—tiny rows like the cornfields. Her gaze falls to a notepad on the table. "These statements. Robert's statements are pretty…it would appear as though he was convinced Jakabie may have intentionally harmed Coty."

I stare at her, my gaze torches through her. I don't hate her and I know she's running on ambition and burnt coffee, but I hate this situation, and right now she's part of it. "He called Jakabie a monster. He said he was a murderer and then he fucking…they both shot and killed themselves. I'd say they were convinced."

She looks up. "I'm so sorry, Drake."

"Don't. Don't apologize to me. Just bring her home. I'm in hell right now, you know that, right?"

She diverts eye contact. "Jakabie had no real friends? No one that drove?"

"I told you already. Coty and I were Jakabie's only friends."

"And Jakabie could drive effectively."

"Effectively?" I chuckle. The morning I spent attempting to teach him to drive my stick-shift the previous summer was as rough on my truck as it was on my nerves. A valiant effort, and an entire morning's worth of determination, but ultimately, I taught him to drive the automatic BMW. Freedom was there that day. It was wide and brilliant in his smile as we crept down the dirt roads. His death-grip on the wheel left his knuckles blanched white atop it. The open road reflected in the darks of his eyes as he stared it down in accomplishment…and then we increased our speed from two miles an hour to five, and then ten. That was a good day. *Was*. Now the memory is poison in my brain. "Yes. He could drive an automatic."

"We've questioned the surrounding neighbors. All vehicles, including recreational vehicles, are accounted for."

"Jakabie grew up in that house…on that land. He knows the area but he's never left it. He doesn't know anything outside the Panhandle. There's only so many miles and he's one kid. You should have found him by now."

"Drake." She leans forward. "We have cadaver dogs, two state agencies, air-crew, and volunteers looking. We have surveyors preparing a geographic map of any abandoned well sites within a ten-mile radius."

"Oh my god." My esophagus quivers at the thought of my daughter's cold, battered body lying lifeless at the bottom of some long-forgotten well. Thoughts of the things that would have happened prior to her being thrown there are revolting and excruciating. *And I am officially one of those parents.*

"My intention is not to upset you but to be open with you. We're coming up on thirty hours. We are mobilized."

"So what? I just sit here and wait until you find her?" My throat tightens.

"No. Ashlyn is here. We have your contact information and you have ours. We know her address and how to find you if needed. Rest. If I find something, you will be the first person I call."

The feet of the chair rub loudly across the cement floor as I scoot back to stand.

"Drake. What you saw today was traumatic. If you need help processing that, we can—"

"A man told me his son, a kid I care very much about, murdered my five-year-old daughter." I look down on a scowled Salizar as I stand. "What happened afterward was a walk in the park."

The lobby of the Police Station feels like a stage—all eyes on me as I walk to Ashlyn in defeat. I feel myself disintegrating as I near her. The instant her soft hand rests aside my face, I'm obliterated. My wailing fills the lobby as she embraces me briefly before leading me out to her vehicle.

There's a mutual silence on the drive to her home. I stare blankly out the passenger window, contemplating how I'll frame the conversation with Renee. Most days I don't hate Renee. As much as I want to hate her each and every day, I can't. To be honest, I'm unsure if I knew what true hatred was, what it looked like and how it hurt until now.

I think Renee loves with all she has; unfortunately, that isn't much. Of course, as her ex-husband, I'm convinced she's entirely selfish—although, Renee has never been a materialistic person. She loved me and Coty with what she could, and then she left us for a new life. Perhaps some people are emotionally wired in a way which makes no sense to the rest of us. Still, knowing I'm to have to tell her of Coty's disappearance and hear the pain in her voice has me writhing inside. As we turn onto Main Street, I press call and lift my phone.

*"Hello?"*

"Sherri?"

Sherri is Renee's mother. I call her…she calls Renee, and Renee calls me. This process was decreed some time ago in an effort to keep the disruption of Renee's new life at a minimum.

*"Drake. Are you well, dear? Is DeCota well?"*

"Sherri," my voice fails me momentarily, "I need Renee to call me immediately. It's an emergency."

*"Oh dear. Drake, is it DeCota?"*

"Yes. Sherri…something happened."

Renee's parents have always been cordial, yet they've never been a part of Coty's life. They met her briefly in Boston after she was born, but have only seen her through Facetime on occasion since then. It's as if they're horrified of leaving the safety of Quebec.

The few times I've spoken with Sherri in person proved to be awkward. She seems to lack the ability to display basic emotion. Now, she's somewhat distraught as I tell her what I know and five minutes later, Renee is calling me.

*"Drake. Hello?"*

"Renee?"

*"Drake…what, what is going on? Please tell me this is some sad dream."*

"It's Coty. She's missing."

*"What? It's true?"* She and a man are speaking French in a side conversation.

*"Drake, I am on holiday in Singapore. We can leave promptly."* Her voice courses with concern. It cracks and quivers through the connection.

"Wait. Renee…there isn't much to do from here but pace. Ren…Renee."

*"What is it, Drake?"*

"I think this is bad."

I hear choppy inhalation on the other end. *"How…how bad, Drake?"*

*"She's gone, Renee. I think she's gone."*

There's commotion, rustling, and perhaps screaming before the phone goes dead.

I remain seated in Ashlyn's car in her driveway. She lives in a small yellow house with a tire swing hanging from a large tree branch in the front yard. She has no nieces or nephews and I've never seen a single child in her neighborhood. Perhaps she swings at night when no one is watching. I'm in no mood to ask so I sit, watching it. It taunts me, slightly swaying with the breeze. Coty will never sit there, giggling with a Popsicle grin as I push her. *Will Coty really never sit there? Is she really gone forever? My daughter is gone. Coty is dead—*

"Lunch is on the table, bubba."

"Huh?"

"Let's go inside. I've made us some burgers—"

"I can't eat. I can't do anything right now."

"Let's go. It's probably already cold."

Sitting at the table is misery. As if I'm chewing tar and cardboard, each piece of food I place in my mouth is more disgusting than the one before it. She watches me. I'd rather choke it down than argue…or talk.

"Will Renee's parent's come here too?"

I shrug.

"When do you imagine she'll be here?"

Again, I shrug.

"'Kay. After you eat I'll draw you a bath and you can nap afterward."

Shaking my head, I look to my plate. "I need to be doing something."

"Drake. You are doing something. Right now you're taking care of yourself and letting the authorities do their job."

"I'm full."

She eyes my half-eaten burger before standing and taking my plate. "I'll run your water."

In her bathroom, I step into the cast-iron tub. The water's so hot it is nearly unbearable but I continue to slide in until my pecs are submerged. A few seconds later she enters with some jar and some incense thing.

On a stool next to the tub, she pushes me forward and rubs my back with a coarse piece of sponge. The scent of something woody fills the air as I close my eyes.

"The son of a librarian and a dermatologist. Came out here from Boston to play with pigs. Such a life, Dr. Graves. I'm one lucky—"

"You're leaving out the part about my parents being dead and now my daughter. It's isn't *such a life*. I'm in a nightmare right now, Ashlyn…one I'll never have the luxury of waking from." Sitting up in the tub, my words leave the only person I have left on the verge of tears. "I'm…I'm sorry."

"Don't be." Her defeated whisper further fragments my broken heart.

"No…you're all I have."

"You don't know that for certain, Drake. Until you know for absolute certain, don't discredit your gut feelings."

"Ashlyn, the Mathews didn't *kill* themselves for something insignificant. He called him a murderer and he wouldn't even look me in the eyes while he said it." I shake my head. "I said he wouldn't hurt her. But a week ago I'd have said you were crazy if you told me Jakabie Mathews had broken into my house and…"

I stare at Ashlyn.

"What…Drake. What is it?"

"Ashlyn. You can't so much as turn a small circle anywhere in that house without the floors bellyaching and creaking. It's impossible to sneak through that place unnoticed. How didn't we hear Jakabie come in or Coty go out?"

"I don't…I don't know, Drake. I do know that I've never once been to your house when your front door has been locked. And you've said that Coty could sleep through a hurricane. We weren't expecting Jakabie to come in. You'd just taken him home earlier."

I return my gaze to the water as she continues washing over my back. "I've done a few things right in life. But she was perfect. She was my perfection."

Post bath, my skin is steaming and red and the heat fuels my exhaustion. Ashlyn has hung thick blankets over her bedroom windows and the room is as dark as midnight minus the moon and stars. I slide under cool, comforting sheets. Ashlyn kisses my cheek before leaving me in the darkness. A few tears tickle my nose as they make their way down, and then I fade.

A rattling on the walls and my skull has me flinging bedsheets from me, sitting upright and wondering where the hell I am. I can't see, so I remain still until light floods in from the bedroom door.

"Drake. Get up." Ashlyn rushes to the bedside.

It's only now I realize I've woken up at Ashlyn's. "Did they find her?"

"No. The police are here. They need to talk with you."

Shaky, my knees feel frail. I stand in the kitchen in front of two officers I've not met yet previously.

A Hispanic officer in his twenties produces an iPad, showcasing pictures. I stare in disbelief as he scrolls through images of my daughter's personal belongings. A Doc McStuffins' t-shirt, socks, and a pair of shorts of Coty's from when she was much younger appear on the screen in separate pictures.

"Dr. Graves, are these your daughter's things?"

"Yes."

"They were in a box under Jakabie Mathews' bed."

My eyes glisten. My butt rests against the countertop as I stare at the wall with my hand clasped over my mouth.

"Graves—"

"Just find my daughter!"

The officer steps back. "There's more."

"More? What the hell do you mean?"

We sit at the table. I'm sure my grip on Ashlyn's hand is overbearing but I can't let go. The officers produce a drawing of stick figures within a transparent evidence bag. The simple drawing showcases two stick people—one figure is small and sad, the other is large and hovering…touching the smaller one where it should not be touched. The picture appears to have been folded and unfolded several times.

"It would appear as though Coty was attempting to communicate the abuse, Dr. Graves, but didn't know how."

"You found this in his room, too?" My voice is a whisper.

"No. Hers."

I release Ashlyn's hand. The chair crashes to the floor behind me as I stand and rush from the kitchen and to the bathroom to purge the meal I'd eaten earlier. Hovering over the toilet, gagging, I find I'm wanting to hurt myself—physically. I want to inflict pain for allowing my daughter to have suffered and to have been so incredibly blind to that suffering. Thoughts of what she must have gone through before her demise have me dry-heaving.

"No!" I glare at my reflection in the water below me. I'm shit, so this feels appropriate, seeing my face here. No more stillness.

I return to the kitchen, unsure if it's motivation, rage, or a combination of emotions which are unclassifiable at this point and look at a teary scene. "No more standing still. I'm going with the volunteers. I'm finding her. I'm going to help bring Coty home."

Their faces harden as if they might oppose, yet nothing is vocalized.

Ashlyn stands. "I can go, too."

The officers finish their mugs of coffee rapidly from

the table as if that will buy them a few seconds to formulate a response.

"Just stay clear the yellow tape, same as everyone else."

We arrive at my farmhouse thirty minutes later. It's not my home. It's not even my world. Examining my property from Ashlyn's vehicle across the road, it's as if I'm viewing a living magazine page or a snowless snow-globe.

People on my porch and casually meandering about my yard leave me feeling detached. The yellow tape catches the sun's glare as it bounces on the breeze— stretched out between thin posts. It's disgusting.

"There's Officer Salizar." Ashlyn's hand rests on my thigh as my gaze lingers past Salizar and lands on the Mathews' home.

"She never sleeps," I mumble.

The vehicles here today look meaner. Their windows are the deepest black and are highly intimidating as if someone were to be snatched up into one of the vans, the world outside would be clueless about the happenings within.

The chopping reverberations beating down on the vehicle remind me at least two helicopters hover above, looking for my daughter.

"Are you sure you want to do this? They've already walked the area with the dogs."

"I can't just *be*, Ashlyn. I have to do something."

August is merciless. The heat index leaves us cowering the instant we step out of the car. The sky is cloudless, no shadows cast for relief from the pelting rays above.

Salizar is walking to us within seconds of us making

our way to the front of the Honda.

"Hope you brought water. It's the Devil's den out here." Sweat streams the heavy creases of her face.

"How does this work? Am I supervised to walk around my own property?"

Salizar places her hands on her hips. Her scowl forms instantly. "Why do you need to walk around? I told you we'd let you know as soon as it was okay to return." The wet stains under either armpit assure me she's been in the elements a while.

"I want to help with the volunteer efforts. I need to help look."

"They're gone, Drake. The only people covering ground now are professional investigators."

It's only now I'm noticing I recognize no one. "So I have to leave? I can't just look around?"

Her scowl retreats. "What for? We've covered the area. The things we're looking for now are the things we can't see with the naked eye."

I nod. "It's just, I know her. I knew her best. And every hour that passes I feel further from her. I just want to walk around. Please. I might be able to do some good. Or at least do me some good."

She heaves, looking around to those looking back at us from the porch and vehicles parked on my lawn. They stare as though I'm the trespasser. "You don't go past that tape without an escort. You'll be back in your home tonight or early tomorrow morning, anyway."

"Yes, ma'am."

Sweat cascades down my legs from inside my jeans. It feels as though the sun is only minutes away from baking my brain within my skull.

Skimming the area, I attempt to quell my emotion as

thoughts of Coty running about the property happily are inevitably invading. Tiny numbered flags dot the yard. They mark little tidbits that may or may not be clues.

Little stones and twigs crunch like cornflakes as I walk aimlessly to the open backyard. It's the only area without yellow tape and mined with red flags. The remains of an antique tractor and a rusted T-shaped clothesline pole have been resting for what appears to be ages in the furthest corner of the east end of the backyard.

Ashlyn on my heels, I stop just next to the remaining rubber of the tractor tire. Tall weeds surround the structure and it stands only waist high.

I rarely saw Coty here while playing outside. The area is known for rattlesnakes. For some reason, however, I feel close to my daughter while standing here. Looking over the property, I imagine it without the flags and yellow tape—I imagine how it looked just two days ago. I skim over objects, selecting things Coty has 'spied' in the past. So much love and history compacted into so little time.

"You could get some money from this thing." Ashlyn taps the tractor with her foot.

"Yeah. Whoever buys this place next can keep it all." I turn, resting my elbows on the crumbling rubber.

"Drake…we have memories to make here. You, me, and—"

"Please…Ashlyn. I can't do this now."

A mild breeze offers a brief reprieve. My attention is snared by the rusty toolbox secured in place beneath what's left of the tractor seat on the floor. My curiosity of its contents has me reaching for the rusted latch. It's surprisingly easy to open.

Opening the lid, I gaze upon a green Zip-Lock baggy—certainly not something from the 1920's era. I see these bags advertised on TV all the time to reduce freezer burn.

Immediately I'm reaching for it, peeling the bag open rapidly and dumping its contents in the otherwise small and empty toolbox. I'm horrified.

"What is that, Drake?"

"G…get Salizar, please."

Ashlyn steps closer as we look upon the childish drawings. Sketches on worn paper, distinctly similar to the one found in Coty's room, and a Teenage Mutant Ninja Turtle coloring book lying open with pages exposed. The pictures visible aren't colored; however, the crotches of the turtles and April O'Neil have been heavily marked over with what appears to be a black crown.

"Shit! Drake…is that Coty's book? Are those…are those Coty's?"

"I don't…I don't know, Ashlyn. The drawings are the same as the one in Coty's room. They have to be hers." Flipping one of the pictures over, my jaw falls agape as I read, 'Jakabie hates Gary.' The childish letters are large and sloppy, yet clearly readable.

"Sal…Salizar!" Her name tears from my throat like a bandage being ripped away from a healing wound, taking a scab with it. "Please! Officer!"

We're surrounded in seconds and gently pushed away from the tractor. "Who the fuck is Gary?" I hear myself asking repeatedly.

Mumbles, headshakes, and blank stares have me wanting to knock the entourage of officers away from my find like a bowling ball right through the center.

"Who the *fuck* is Gary?"

"I don't know!" Salizar turns to me.

"Then why are you still standing there?" My hands go up and then fall down to my side. "If Jakabie drew those pictures and the picture you found in Coty's room, then that means Coty didn't. That's a game changer." I point at them in an effort to drive my point. A flutter of hope is tiptoeing up through my chest, curling my lips.

Salizar is motioning me to step back while summoning people from the parked van.

"Told you." The flutter is now a resurgence.

"Told me what, Drake?" Salizar seems somewhere between irritated and excited.

"That I might do some good."

An hour later I'm seated like a guest at my own bistro table in my own kitchen. The toolbox findings only multiply questions. Scenarios are played out in my mind, yet each of them lead me back to 'why.' Why did Jakabie take Coty?

My heels bounce nervously on the floor beneath my chair—hands clasped as I chew relentlessly on my thumb. The kitchen is thick with scuffling officers but the only one I care to see is Salizar.

Ashlyn sits across from me, placing her hand on my forearm. "This was a good find, Drake."

The worthless officer, Nathan, eats Doritos from my cabinet while complaining to fellow officers about his recent Taco Bell order. He's portly and pungent, like a mound of minced onions. Amidst this all, I find myself hoping he chokes.

Finally, Salizar returns. "Well, son." She stands over us. "I found Gary."

Eyes widening, I shrug, prompting her to continue. "Gary Fiddler was a nursing attending at the Manor where Jakabie's grandmother resided until her passing."

"Okay." I look to Ashlyn, the confusion in my voice matches that on her face.

"Fiddler the diddler. That's the name he was given after he was caught with a young girl in the janitor's closet on Easter Sunday. An investigation showed that Gary Fiddler had assaulted at least two little girls and four little boys…one of them being Jakabie."

"Oh my god." Ashlyn shakes her head.

"What's worse…Jakabie is thought to have suffered the brunt of the abuse because he was mute until the age of six." Salizar exhales. "The full extent of his abuse was captured over time…in pictures and tidbits of stories as he gained the ability to communicate with his voice. By that time, Fiddler had succumbed to alcoholic cirrhosis in prison—nasty bastard."

I stand, my elbows in the air as my hands rest behind my head. "So, what does this mean for Coty? It sucks…I don't mean to sound insensitive, but what's done is done. What does this mean for my daughter if she didn't draw the picture?"

She sighs heavily. "Drake, it only means she didn't draw that picture. The reality is, we still have no idea where they are and tomorrow morning we'll be at forty-eight hours. We found personal clothing items under Jakabie's bed and the sad reality is, many children who have been violated grow up to be repeat offenders."

"So, this actually makes it worse. Now we know why he's capable."

"Knowledge is power," Salizar mutters, "but only

when it doesn't leave you defenseless. Be rational, but remember we don't have a body, Graves. Until you know for certain—"

"Oh…my god." It hits me. *Robert knew.* "Growing monsters…Robert knew what Jakabie was doing to Coty all along. He had to have known. He knew where they were and he and Maurine both knew what he was doing to my daughter!"

"Drake." Ashlyn stands as I walk from the kitchen and out the front door. "Drake, wait."

"Where the hell is she, Ashlyn?" I turn to her. "I just want to tell her I'm sorry for not knowing and put her to rest."

In the heat, the Devil's den, the hope within me withers and fades like the tiny yellow wildflowers along our country roads in late summer. "How could I have not known, Ashlyn?"

"Drake…" Her soft hands rest on either side of my face. "The sickest people on this earth are also the best pretenders. That's what makes them so sick. This isn't your fault. You were and are an excellent father. Always believe that."

We're joined by Salizar. Her thin lips stiffen, as though a word is stuck between them. Just before it escapes, I beat her to it.

"What's the plan. Here and now." I stomp. "I'm done waiting. Your entire bullshit operation is here at *my* house. Meanwhile, I'm displaced, and I think it's pretty fucking obvious that Coty isn't here or anywhere around here, so what are you going to do now?"

Salizar's nostrils flare. "What makes you think our efforts are localized to here alone, son? And aren't you sitting pretty with your little girlfriend here?"

Scanning the area, I look once more to the sky. "I was wrong, I guess. Little girls do just evaporate."

"No, Drake, they don't. That's why we're knocking on every door and plan on searching in every barn and shed. We won't stop."

"I can't wait anymore—"

"You don't gotta choice! Jakabie Mathews is one boy. *One!*" Salizar steps forward, her index finger erected and in my face. "He has limited resources and nowhere to go. We will find him."

I exhale forcefully, stepping even closer in her direction. "I have no doubt you will find him, Officer. My question is why the *fuck* haven't you already?"

Ashlyn and I escape the high temperature's tyranny, the pictures, and the horde of investigators by returning to her small car and driving away. We leave without a specific destination, driving down dusty backroads. She seems to have the same idea as I do. Our gazes scan the area for abandoned houses and barns; the plains are riddled with them. Surely this team of investigators couldn't have effectively searched each structure here.

"I thought it might be impossible to hide out here…or at least to stay hidden. But now I just don't know."

"What if they never bring her home, Ashlyn? I don't think I can feel this way every day. How do parents do this? Those stories on the TV, how do parents who lose their kids go the rest of their lives without closure?"

Miles and minutes later, we approach the outskirts of town. Because my practice is on the highway going into town, I've asked Ashlyn if we can stop by briefly before returning to her place.

My veterinary clinic is a second home. One of

Coty's favorite things to do was inventory. I have no clue what she found so interesting about counting medications and surgical products. She loved interacting with the customers who purchased wormers and other treatments from the clinic.

We walk in and the place smells stale and musty, like when I first opened the doors.

"Maybe we can freshen up in here. It might take some frustration out." Ashlyn props the door open with the red brick, letting in hot, fresh air.

"Come here," I softly summon her.

Taking her into my arms, I hold tightly the only person I have left. She has no ties to me. She could leave me stranded in a sea of people who owe me nothing. *I have no family.* "When this is over, Ashlyn, when we find her, I'm going to need help. I'm going to need you."

"I know that."

"If this is too much…I understand if this is just too—"

"Stop." She pushes off just enough to make eye contact. "I'm not going anywhere unless you ask me to." She kisses my chin. "Isn't it obvious? I've only been pursuing you relentlessly because I clearly have an agenda, Drake. I love you. And I'm going to be here with you on the other side of this, no matter what that looks like, okay?"

"Okay."

We release one another and I reach for the air-freshener from under the counter, spraying the stuffy atmosphere while she grabs the dust rags. It's not long and the front office is looking presentable again.

My phone pulsates rapidly, as does my heart when I

look to see Salizar's name on my screen. Ashlyn's pupils scan my face as Salizar tells me only that I'm free to return home when I'm ready. She says nothing of my daughter's whereabouts.

We continue the clean-up before creeping back down the dirt road an hour or so later.

"Are you sure it's okay? My boss said I can take as much time as I need."

I take her hand. "Go do nursing stuff tonight. It might do you some good. I'm going to clean up and, I dunno. I don't know what I'm going to do. I'll be fine."

The car slinks down the drive. There's a dark van on my lawn still, and the yellow tape is glaring at me as if I'm intruding as we creep past.

I slam the door and wave goodbye…watch her drive away and leave me to my new life. I'm half-expecting my house and everything in it to be tossed and thrown about chaotically. Again, the cop shows I watch have proven to be a gross exaggeration. Inside, my house smells of other men's colognes and body washes. In the kitchen, dishes are cleaned and drying on the rack rather than in the washer.

An odd feeling of unfamiliarity has me rigid as if I'm invading another home and life. This is another life and the home is a shell of memories. Perhaps one day I'll cherish these precious recollections, but for now, they're taunting me from every angle. Coty is captured, year by year, on the walls within frames. Her toys and books are placed neatly where they are supposed to go before bedtime.

Many mornings I'd spend cleaning tiny hand and face prints from the large glass window behind the couch. As I look at them now, knowing they'll be the last, I find myself unable to cope. I'm alone, so I allow the tears to stream and make my way to the kitchen. I grab a black marker from the junk drawer and return to the window, drawing a large square around Coty's smudges. I want them there for as long as possible.

The last time she was here she spied the scarecrow…she saw Jakabie. *Had I only known.*

The stairs squawk and squeak as I ascend.

Countless times I've made my way to the top and it was meaningless. The wood would moan beneath my weight as I trampled up and down doing loads of laundry, picking up stuffed ponies and other toys. With each step, the house is crying with me. Not that the requisite of falling on her bed and screaming *why* hasn't crossed my mind, but as odd as it may seem, I simply crave her scent.

In the mornings, I'd start Coty's day off with baby-bear hugs and papa-bear kisses. The kiddie shampoo she used smelled like watermelon and I had to use a certain fabric softener for her skin. The scent combination is her signature smell. Perhaps it lingers on her pillows and bedding.

Just as I reach her room, I opt to return to the kitchen for a drink instead. I can't sink my soul any further right now. It's resting wretchedly at its lowest depth. Five o'clock is every hour for a parent in my condition.

Alcohol is a trickster. Sipping my Coke and rum, I glance out the large window from the couch. One second, the rum grants permission to smile when her giggle tickles my memory. Seconds later, I'm bitch-slapped with guilt for allowing myself to feel anything other than complete depletion. Two large glasses in and I'm done. I'm woozy and more than certain that no matter what I poison myself with, it's all going to be here when I wake up.

I lie back on the couch, staring at the ceiling. I close my eyes. Perhaps tonight I'll sail the seas…or perhaps tonight she'll come to me and I'll hold her…kiss her sweet face and tell her how thankful I was to have been her daddy…*chase my dreams like fireflies*.

She's calling to me. Her voice is stifled through stalks of tall corn, but somewhere within the crop…Coty is calling out my name…*Daddy*.

The sky above swirls and gives a thunderous chuckle. It's painted purple, black, and dark gray…the kind of beauty one might only appreciate from the safety of indoors.

"Coty!"

Her tiny voice dances atop the numerous plants and leaves me unable to pinpoint where she's calling from. The insidious sky assures me I don't have the luxury of strategizing. It's only when I attempt to lift my foot that I realize it's firmly anchored to the soil beneath it. *What is this cruelty?*

"Coty! Come to me!" Looking once more to my sneakers, I'm horrified to see they're speckled with blood.

On either side of me, Maurine and Robert Mathews stand, gazing out over their field. They both bear ghastly gunshot wounds to their heads, which are bleeding profusely.

"I'm dreaming. No! Coty! Coty, please. I want…let me hold you!"

"All God's children," Robert mutters.

My limbs are compromised; I'm unable to punch the bastard in the face while he stares expressionless, listening to Coty's calls.

"He holds them all," Maurine follows up.

"Fuck both of you. Coty!"

A rustling from just a few rows within the crop has me kneeling. My breath escapes me as my precious daughter pushes the stalks from her path and steps from the cornfield to me.

In my arms, finally. I know this reunion is a gift from my mind, but I'll take it. Right now I'm holding her and hearing her breathe.

"I'm so sorry, Coty!"

As she pushes away, I notice the Mathews are no longer with us. We're alone and under a bright blue sky…it no longer boasts a sinister agenda.

"No, Daddy. It's okay." Her little hand wipes a tear away just before our world is fractured.

# Chapter Six

It's black. I'm yanked from slumber and the company of my daughter by some familiar sound, yet my mind doesn't initially register its origin. My phone is sounding off in the darkness but the tune is something odd. I hate it. Thoughts of smashing it into a million pieces have me frantically searching for it. Coty's scent, her smile, was mine for but a brief moment and this goddamned phone has stolen that from me. Whoever is responsible will be left speechless after I press answer.

Device in hand, I realize the tone isn't a text, email, or some social media alert. It's a breach alert from my security system. Immediately I sit up on the couch, scanning the living room, but the area is completely dark. The idea that someone might be lurking in my home has me locked up. A second glance and a few more moments of revival show the alert isn't regarding an entry or potential entry to my home, but to the clinic.

"What the—"

I yelp, dropping my phone as a Cat Stevens ringtone blares through my hollow-sounding house. The security company is calling me.

"Hello?" I frantically answer once I've collected my thoughts and phone.

*"Mr. Graves?"*

"Yes."

*"Hello. This is KZ security. Can you verify with your special word?"*

"Yeah, it's…firefly."

*"Excellent. I see there's activity at location B?"*

"Yes. I was there earlier. I think I didn't lock the door and wind caught it. I'm heading there now."

*"Actually, Mr. Graves, KZ always recommends the appropriate authorities respond to situations where home and business owners aren't there to verify there isn't an invasion. It's simply for your safety."*

I chuckle. "I'm not dealing with any appropriate authorities tonight. If I notice anything suspicious I'll call my buddies in blue."

*"Mr. Graves—"*

"Bye now."

I find my keys, grab my small handgun from the closet shelf, and make my way out the door. It's already ten in the evening. The sky is starless, I'm assuming blanketed in clouds. I feel blanketed, too. My head's foggy.

Replaying my actions from earlier, I find I'm becoming increasingly concerned that this breach alert isn't from the wind. I'm certain we locked the door prior to leaving. Tranquilizers and narcotics are locked away within a secure area, so there's really no reason for burglary. The clinic has no cash reserves stored away. Only another veterinarian or someone who knows the black market vet supply would benefit from taking anything from me.

Minutes later, I'm there. Perhaps there's uncertainty surrounding whether or not Ashlyn and I locked the front door, but being energy conscious as I am, I know I'm not responsible for the light glaring at me out of the window from the back of the building.

Gun in hand, I make my way to the door to find it locked. Perhaps it's stupidity, perhaps it's anger, or maybe it's just because I legitimately don't give a damn anymore. Something has me unlocking the door and walking in rather than calling the police.

Inside, the front area appears unviolated. I enter Coty's birthday backward into the keypad near the door, disabling the silent alarm, and slide down the hall cautiously toward the light. *Perhaps Ashlyn flipped it on and I didn't catch it.*

The back room of the clinic houses a small fridge, microwave, and cheap seating for four—a *makeshift kitchen*. There's nothing there worth taking. Just before I around the corner, a faint breeze brushes past me. The air is summer-kissed, yet it has me shivering. There are odd little tapping noises and I immediately envision the intruder tapping his or her foot on the floor.

Swallowing hard, taking full advantage of the fact that I have nothing to lose, I round the corner to see an open back window. It taps gently under the command of the Oklahoma wind. I search my memory. The day's cleaning efforts were inclusive of airing the building out. I distinctly remember Ashlyn saying she was going to let the air flow through and my head was on a different planet at the time. It all makes sense now. The window tripped the alarm when the wind blew it open. Ashlyn left the light on and this was all a misunderstanding. I lower the gun, lock the window, and pull out a flimsy chair.

Coty and I have had so many lunches at this little table. She loved animals but was insistent on being a princess when she grew up, not a vet. *She was a princess.*

I look in the direction of the fridge. For an instant, I remind myself to grab strawberry jelly the next time I'm in town…but then I'm sucked back into a different reality—the present reality. I don't like jelly. Only Coty likes jelly. *I'll never need to buy jelly again…*

I glance at three cut bread crusts on the countertop and for a second the sight of them does nothing. Then I stand, stare, and nearly hyperventilate. The crusts lie cut on the off-white Formica countertop of the clinic kitchen. Three crusts…the way Jakabie eats his sandwiches.

"Jak…Jakabie!" I yell out. Running down the hall, I flip on each light in the place. "Jakabie, are you in here? Where are you?"

Bolting from the front door, I encircle the building, yelling out his name. There's no one there. Nothing is here but proof of his existence. He's alive and he's close. He holds all the answers, even if my ears and heart can't bear to hear them. Only he can tell me why he did this and where she is. He can release me from this anxiety so that I might be able to grieve appropriately for the remainder of my miserable life. "Dammit, Jakabie! Where are you!"

He's on foot. That means he must be close.

After thoroughly investigating the premises, shining my iPhone flashlight around brush piles and a stock-trailer, I jump in my truck. Rather than racing, I set my pace down the highway, looking for any movement along the sides of the road.

My foot dances atop the gas pedal nervously and my thoughts are as scattered as the dead vegetation on either side of the stretch of highway. Attempts to call Ashlyn are futile. I know working nights at the hospital means she can't answer her phone when she's with a patient.

Once I've driven the highway in either direction and have seen nothing but fleeing field mice and jackrabbits, I call Salizar.

Initially, she sounds put off with my hastily prepared proclamation. It isn't until I slow my speech and explain to her why this event is so impactful that she too gains excitement. I'm instructed to wait at the clinic, in my locked vehicle for their arrival.

The squad cars arrive just as the stars do. The night is slightly brighter.

Hours pass and the area is swarmed with headlights. It's as if we're searching for a ghost who draws sad pictures and hates crusts.

There is a renewed hope in the idea that he might be stationed somewhere close to the clinic, even if it's for the night. We're at least fifteen miles from my house, so it would have taken him a while to walk this distance. *He was running*. Jakabie loves to run. I wonder where my baby is and what I'll have to lay to rest.

I offer Salizar a warm bottle of water while we stand in the front area of the clinic. She's holding something emotionally taxing. Her expression and posture assure me she has some form of information.

"What is it? Did you find something tonight? Did

one of your men…"

She smiles, swallowing. "Young man, this wasn't the only call we received tonight."

"What? What do you mean? Did you find her—"

"No. No, we didn't. Let me finish." Her head cocks, her gaze is stern yet soft. "The hog farm…there's a hog farm just up the way."

"I know. I drive by it every day."

"We got an anonymous call, Drake." It's apparent that whatever she's needing to say is dreadfully difficult. "Just after I hung up with you, Special Agent Alvarado called. Said someone driving past the pig barns called in with a tip." She stares at me. Her eyes are pained. She's desperate to leap past these next few moments."

"Dammit, Salizar! Just tell me!"

"They saw a man tonight, Graves. They saw a man under the lights, toting something around the sewage lagoon. They watched him heave it in. They were certain it was…certain it was…"

"No! I'll kill him. I'll fucking kill him. Who called this in? Is it a legitimate—"

"She was Spanish-speaking and claimed to be an undocumented citizen. She remained anonymous for obvious reasons, but said she had to tell someone what she saw."

"Oh my god…what, what are you going to do?"

"We're there now, son. The crew and the barn management are searching the area. It's not as if we can drag a tarped lagoon, and Alvarado said even the mention of searching the goddamned thing has got their big dogs' panties twisted up. Either way, this woman was convinced and she had no reason to lie."

"No. That sonofabitch!"

"Listen to me! Please do not go all cowboy and do something stupid. The last thing you need right now is to get arrested. We can't say for certain the man was Jakabie or what he tossed was…"

"He was just here! We have proof!" The image of Coty sinking is swine sewage—my daughter's legacy: kidnapped, violated, murdered, and tossed in a pond of pig shit? "You think I give a *fuck* about being arrested? Do you have any idea the things I'm going to do to him when I find him? Your worst crime scene will look like child's play when I'm done. Are you hearing me—"

*"Graves!"* Her eyes bulge in rage. "You listen to me. I can't imagine what you're going through right now but—"

"No, you can't! Until you have lost a child to some sadistic bastard you invited into your own home, don't tell me how to feel or what to do."

She nods. "I don't know how you feel because every loss is different. But I'm no stranger to the ache of child loss. My son was four when he took that stranger's hand. Why do you think I picked up this fucking badge? It's not for the paycheck, Graves."

*Connection.*

"I will bring your daughter home or die trying. I promise you that. But you have to know that there aren't any wands in my toolbox. I'm trying with all I have. We all are. And when this is done, I want you to be able to recover without anything in the way of that. So, no. You aren't killing anybody. You're going to let me do my job…I'll kill that motherfucker." She smiles.

As much as I hurt, I smile back. For the first time during this agonizing process, I'm confident I won't spend my days wondering where my daughter is resting unpeacefully. "What do I do? I'm lost."

"I need you to go home and be with the ones you love. Don't be alone. Surround yourself with support."

"Okay." As if on cue, Ashlyn's number is on my screen.

"Hello?"

*"Hey, sugar-bear. Sorry I missed your call."* An alarm beeps in the background. *"I've had a crazy night."*

"Me too. I'm glad it's almost over."

I didn't re-enter my home when I returned at nearly five in the morning. Instead, I've been sitting on the porch, rocking in my chair. Coty's little pink chair will rock occasionally too in the sporadic gusts of hot morning wind.

Ashlyn's car comes into view and with it a feeling of comfort. *Ashlyn feels like coming home.*

She exits the vehicle, her eyes puffy and red as she walks to me. Neither of us says anything, we simply embrace on the porch and weep.

She kisses my cheek. "We both smell horrible. Let's go shower."

Salizar said she'd notify me the instant the lagoon search showed anything—if it showed anything. She also stated if the initial walk around yielded nothing, searching the lagoon would require coordination and she couldn't offer specific timelines.

In the bathroom, water running and heating, neither of us say anything as we undress. It's a funny thing. When there's nothing left to do, one is simply silent. I want to crawl into bed and hide from the world but my world has been shattered and I have to find out why he threw the rock. I want to scream and cry and, "let it all out," but the reality is that there's nothing to let out…it's part of me now. My pain will forever be a part of my definition. Screaming does nothing. There's nothing to do but stand nude in water with the only other human on the planet that brings me comfort. So that's what we do.

We wash. The steam and water rejuvenate my skin and scratchy eyes but do nothing for me internally. Then we hold one another until the heat in the water is gone.

Dried and sporting underwear alone, we sit in the kitchen.

"I need you to know something." Her words break the silence.

Ashlyn is most beautiful when she's tired. There's something about her eyes and the way she glows when she's moments away from giving in to her exhaustion.

"Okay. Then tell me." I smile.

"I know today is going to hurt, just like yesterday. I'm sure tomorrow won't feel any better. It might hurt worse. But eventually, the pain is going to ease just enough that you'll be able to breathe without hurting."

I take her hand.

"Drake, you're all I have, too…I mean, other than my worthless brother."

We chuckle.

"You're my family, Drake. I need you just as much as you need me. I can't lose you either. I refuse to."

Her words are an instant relief. The thought of losing her is unfathomable.

We curl up in bed, snuggled next to each other. Sleep comes hard and fast and unavoidable.

# Chapter Seven

"When did you know? Like, when were you certain it was just over?" Ashlyn's question is asked over a shared bowl of yogurt and granola at nearly two in the afternoon. We'd slept the morning away and were now listening to the rains return outside. Forty-eight hours was a few hours back. I've decided to stop counting.

"Hmmm. I guess I didn't. With her, I never really knew what normalcy was. We were just us. So, when it was done it was just abruptly over and she was gone."

"Do you think she regrets what she did? Do you think she'll look back and wonder what might have been?"

I set my spoon down, contemplating how to put my thoughts into words. "I think we'll all wonder that, even if our choices aren't so obviously poor. With Renee, I don't know if she had it in her to be a mom and a wife. I think she tried with what she had, but ultimately, she was never one to be something or try to be something she wasn't. So, she stopped."

"Do you think she wanted to be a mom and then changed her mind?"

The day Renee set the pregnancy test in front of me was one of the happiest days of my life. It was also one of the loneliest because I was isolated in my joy. The pregnancy was a mishap, but even then, she acted as though it was a horrendous diagnosis rather than a tiny life. Renee knew there were options, and she knew I would have been supportive of those options. She chose to have Coty. She chose to leave Boston for Oklahoma, and she chose to leave us for Canada.

"No. I don't think she wanted to be a mother. I don't think Renee's wired like that."

Ashlyn squints. The spoon is upside down in her mouth. She appears to be pondering.

"What?" I ask.

"I just…how did you fall in love with her? You say she never loved you, she was bored with you, and showed little interest in you. She didn't want to be the mother of the child she shared with you…I mean, the bitch sounds awful."

We share a laugh. It feels good to laugh from my belly.

"I didn't know what love was, I guess. I loved her, but I wasn't *in love* with her. We were young and stupid, and she got pregnant, and I guess she saw that as a trap." I sigh. "Maybe I was a trap. After…after the accident she was all I had until Coty came. That couldn't have been an easy burden to bear. Yes, I want to hate her some days for leaving Coty with questions I couldn't answer. But the flip side of that is she also left me the best days of my life. If it wasn't for her I wouldn't have had Coty. How can I hate her?"

She nods. She gets it.

We finish lunch, get dressed, and walk outside to see

the rain has left, leaving behind a bashful sun. It plays peekaboo in the thinning clouds above. Hand in hand, Ashlyn and I walk down the drive and then down the saturated dirt road, in the opposing direction of the Mathews' home, which is still sporting the yellow crime scene tape around its perimeters.

There's a fine, dewy mist on the air and the meadowlarks and pheasants are calling. The serenity is shattered as a squad car comes into view from up the road. Salizar is seen through the windshield as the vehicle comes closer. Whatever they found must have been bad enough she needs to tell me in person.

The car slows, flinging bits of mud from the tires upward, and stops. Salizar exits.

"What is it?" My voice quivers at the thought of what she'll say.

"It's nothing. Not yet anyway." The ground squishes beneath her boots as she steps closer. "I can't tell you how sorry I am that I don't have answers for you."

"You didn't find her? She's not in there?"

Salizar exhales. "Son, the Department of Environmental Quality, the EPA, and the State Department of Health are all dictating how we make our next move. If it was up to me, I'd grab ahold of a couple hundred sump-pumps and drain that thing today. From what we're hearing, it's not going to be that easy."

It's a mixed bag of emotion. I want my daughter recovered. The idea of her lying in septic waste churns my insides. But until I hear those words, until their acidity enters my ears and erodes my soul, I maintain a fragment of faith that she might be breathing somewhere, regardless of what the signs say. "Salizar.

How long are we talking? Are they doing anything now?"

"Oh yes. Every agency involved is actively collaborating as we speak. This thing blew the hell up."

"And there probably isn't any sort of a timeline, I'm assuming?" I ask.

She pouts her lips. "May I be brutal with you? The things I say may scar."

"Scar? Ma'am, I'm all but dead inside."

She draws a deep breath through her nostrils. "We anticipate, with the heat and the biological circumstances…if it was colder it would be one thing, but…well…" She pauses, scanning my face as I scan hers. "Her body, if Coty is in there, her body won't stay on the bottom of the lagoon long. She'll rise, and quickly."

I simply nod, staring past her at the tiny ditch weeds attempting to take advantage of the late summer rain and reach skyward. I remember how pretty the plains look when the spring comes and it rains frequently. My mind frantically hunts for fragments to fixate upon. Butterflies, kidney-beans, *The Big Bang Theory*, Salizar's ear mole…anything but *that* thought. Why there? If he had to take my daughter's life, why leave her floating and rotting like she's waste? I try to shake the visual but it's pointless. "Okay. Thank you."

"I'm sorry, Drake."

Again, I nod as I take Ashlyn's hand.

"I'll be in touch." She smiles at Ashlyn before returning to her vehicle.

The first one hundred feet or so are silent. Head down, I focus on the pebbles being kicked before us, bouncing along the wet earth. Coty loved strange looking rocks. Odd stones of various shapes are in her room along her windowsill. My gaze leaves the dampened dirt just in time for the white stucco of the Mathews' home to snicker at me through the large trees and over the vine-covered chain-link.

"When she comes back," Ashlyn breaks the silence, "when she comes back down this road with answers. I'll be here. Right here."

I pull her into me by the shoulder. "I know." Yet, as the stucco home comes closer, I feel as though it's taunting me. I trusted him and built a friendship with him. I fed him and took him into my home. I loved him, and I never even knew him. I need to know the boy—man who took my daughter from me.

"Ashlyn. I need you to help me with something."

"Of course. Anything."

Arm in arm as we continue walking, my stare remains affixed on the Mathews' home. "I need to find out as much as I can about this kid. I need to dissect each detail until something clicks."

"Okay. Maybe we can get a journal and you can try to recall—"

"I want to go back, Ashlyn. I want to go into his house, his room, and absorb each and every lie. I want to experience as much of where he came from as I can."

She slows, tugging my arm slightly. "Drake. That house is part of an investigation. This investigation."

"I know that, Ash." I face her completely. "They're going to find Coty, and they're going to find Jakabie. When they do I'm going to be left with so many questions, and too much time, and too many channels to try to sort it out. If there is something in that house, anything, that might bring me closer to closure—"

"Drake, I love you, but right now there is a team of investigators attempting to coordinate the retrieval of your daughter's body from an agricultural lagoon. There is absolutely nothing in that house that is going to bring you closure."

I'm stunned. I say nothing and I know she's right. I merely return my gaze to the ground and wait for her cue to continue walking.

"Okay. Fine," she says, shaking her head.

I look at her. "Huh?"

"I get it. Jakabie was an important part of your and Coty's life. When they find the bastard, even if he talks, you don't know if you're ever going to get the answers you need from him."

"Exactly."

She chuckles. "Guess how much this girl loves you."

"How much do you love me?" Thunder cracks and echoes across the sky above us we continue walking.

"To the county jail and back. Wait…is breaking and entering a felony or misdemeanor?"

"I don't know. What's the difference? We're not getting caught, regardless."

"You never know, Drake. Of all the places on earth, Jakabie chose your clinic to bust in and make himself a sandwich. That shows he's not only hungry, but senseless, and limited on resources and places to go. They might be expecting him to do something silly like show back up to his own house. So we need to make damn sure the place isn't being watched when we do this, because the last thing either of us needs is a pair of cuffs on our wrists."

We chuckle and make the turn down the drive.

We're joined by meowing Biggles. "Why not tonight?"

Her head fits perfectly on my shoulder as a few fat drops of rain pelt the ground around us, sending Biggles scattering for the barn.

"Again, do you know how much this girl loves you?"

The night comes quickly. The sun seems to have abandoned us early and retreated under the blanket of soft drizzling rainfall.

Sporting black attire and wearing latex surgical gloves for good measure, we stare out of the living room window toward our destination. The scattered clouds have thickened, concealing even the brightest stars.

"I'm nervous, Drake." Ashlyn clings to my arm.

"You don't have to go. You can keep a lookout from here."

She chuckles. "You can't see anything from here. How am I supposed to keep a lookout? Let's get this over with."

We leave my back door like two sneak-thieves tiptoeing from a gated community. Tall, dead weeds, bowing under the condensation, wrap around our ankles as we attempt to move stealthily.

The sprinkling rain is more bothersome than a hindrance to the operation. Soft and slow, it comes straight down on us. It's nearly warm and rather inviting but it bogs our clothing.

There are no headlights on the highways. Only natural noises surround us. "Hurry, Drake. Let's get in and get out." She's at least ten feet ahead of me.

My socks are uncomfortably wet and squishy in my shoes by the time we reach the chain-link fence. We try the front door just for the hell of it. Of course, it's locked, so we make our way around the house, pressing upward on the aged, wood-framed windows. As we near the back of the home and one of the few remaining windows…the bathroom window, we get lucky. Both the screen and the window open as I push them upward.

The window is at least four feet from the ground and there's no way my butt is fitting through it. I look at Ashlyn. Her shoulders drop defeatedly as she walks to me for a boost.

"It's a left and a straight shot to the front door."

She steps into my clasped hands with her left foot, releasing a heavy sigh. "I'm expecting a honeymoon in Bora Bora two years from tonight."

She doesn't give me a chance to respond as her small hands grip the windowsill ambitiously and she pulls herself upward. I watch her tiny figure slip in and briefly, only momentarily, I allow myself the opportunity to escape the present and entertain the idea of a legitimate future with Ashlyn. One complete with some degree of sustainable happiness.

"Ouch." Her voice brings me back.

"You okay?"

"I'm fine…just…I'm a little scared." Her nervous eyes, big and bright, appear out of the window. I just go out of the door and turn right immediately?"

"Yes. You'll run right into the front door. I'll count to three and we'll head there together."

"Or just go now?" She grins and turns back, disappearing in the black.

I rush to the front door, jumping over dark objects on the ground and maneuvering around bushes until I reach the front. The lock clicks, she pulls, I push, and

I'm inside.

The scent of anything smoky, of stove or gun, is gone. The smell reminds me of my grandparents. It's stale with a hint of odd perfume, the cheap stuff older ladies wear in the store on Sundays.

My hand wraps around her forearm. "His room is just here."

In the dark, I reach for the door handle. It's cool in my grasp. I turn and push and enter his world. Flashlight in hand, I look upon the remnants of Jakabie's existence. The bones of the room are all that remain. The mattress has square and rectangular pieces cut from it, and it is propped against the wall. Each drawer from the chest of drawers has been emptied and they're now standing, domino-style, from largest to smallest along the wall. There are few garments of clothing in the open closet, but the walls are bare.

The brown shag carpet nearest the metal bed frame is also missing pieces, cut in squares with both the carpeting and the padding removed to the subflooring.

"They've taken everything in here, Drake."

The wood-panel walls are peppered with tack holes and fragments of scotch tape but are otherwise clean.

"I know. It's like they boxed his life and took it away."

"Drake," Ashlyn nears the mutilated mattress, "did Coty ever come here with Jakabie? Was she ever unsupervised in his room with him?"

I'm shaking my head before she even finishes her question. Although I had foolishly trusted Jakabie, Robert's belligerent consumption of alcohol wasn't something I wanted my daughter exposed to at such an early age. "No. No, she's never been over here by herself."

"You don't…do you think he brought her here that night? Why would they take pieces of the mattress? He's an eighteen-year-old boy. I'm sure this thing would light up from space under ultraviolet. What could they need from it?"

*She's right.* "Oh my god. And the carpet too. He must have brought her here. Salizar knows so much more than she's telling me. It's no wonder the Mathews blew their fucking brains out…they knew I'd kill them all when I learned the truth."

"Drake." She walks to me. "There's nothing here but fuel for your misery."

"No. There's a basement." I turn for the door before she can respond.

This family has shattered mine, and still, a piece of me feels guilty for entering what's left of their lives. A primal need for justification has me lightly traipsing through the living room and to the doorway to the basement. Basements house mildew, spiders, odd smells, and hopefully this one will hold answers. I'm sure it's fear that has Ashlyn joining me as I descend the shabby steps into the concrete sub-level. A quick pass with the flashlight shows the walls to be cracked like spider veins in various areas, and those cracks are dampened. It's musty and the air is heavy and scented with mothballs and dryer lint.

There are several milk crates with objects and paper files in them. They line the west end of the wall. A treadmill is tucked in the corner holding several garments of clothing on hangers.

"Where would we even start, Drake?"

I shrug. "Just look for whatever jumps out at you."

"If something jumps out at me, I'm screaming and running out of here."

The basement is one large room with exposed plumbing. The pipes peek from the ceiling just low enough that I must duck my head while walking underneath them.

Flashlights in hand, we peer into the crates, looking for anything that may give insight. The truth is, I'm needing the recipe book for monsters. I need to know why Jakabie is what he is and why he did what he did. Was it nature, or was it something in this home? *What rotted his roots?*

"Drake, these are receipts and farming records. There's nothing here."

"We need to keep look—"

"Drake. Two teams of investigators have searched through this home. What makes you think we're going to find something with cheap flashlights that they couldn't find with all the shit that they have to find stuff with? There's nothing here to find."

I say nothing, only lower my light. The beam leaves the wall and the crates and settles on the gray, cement floor, making a tiny full moon only inches from my right Nike shoe.

"I came here with you because I love you…and because I can't even imagine what is going on in that mind of yours, but we're not going to find anything, sugar-bear."

I nod my head in agreement. "Yeah. This is pretty crazy, huh."

She grins. "A tad much."

"Let's go."

We lock up the house and begin walking rather than

running back to my home. The moon and a few stars have come out of hiding. It appears they have chased the rain away.

Damp tumbleweeds are kicked from our path and toads sing to us as they enjoy the soggy countryside. I squeeze her hand. "I feel like tonight is my last night as a father."

My comment has her pace slowing. She glares, biting her bottom lip, staring up at me a moment. "What do you mean?"

I take the time to construct my words and what I meant to say in my mind before delivering my statement. "Like, tonight, right now, I'm a dad. I don't know…" I swallow. "I only know that Coty is missing. There's nothing official in front of me. So right now, I'm a daddy."

"Drake, you—"

"But tomorrow, when I'm officially notified and given all the…the details…" I pause for a moment as we walk slowly. "I won't be a father anymore."

She stops. Pulling back on my hand. "Drake," her expression is soft, "you'll always be her daddy. *Always*. There is nothing, and I mean *nothing,* that will ever change that. It's in your history. It's who you are."

I try to smile, but my face is pulling in the opposite direction. The salt of my tears enters my mouth as they stream my face and over the corners of my lips.

"Drake…" she hugs me, her head to my chest, "we're young. Anything is possible. I know that's not where your head is at right now…but I need you to know that our future is open. We have to heal, but we have so much life ahead of us. You can be called daddy again someday."

I know she's trying to bring me comfort, but the idea of replacing Coty is inconceivable. My comment leaves me feeling selfish as well. This isn't about me and my feelings. It's about Coty.

Coty was abducted from her room, under her father's roof, and taken by someone who loves her. She must have been horrified. She probably cried for me and I wasn't there. She knew cruelty, the darkest of humanity, before she left this earth. Her last moments were saturated with it…and where was I? I was sleeping in bed while the wolf made away with my baby girl. The same wolf I let into my kingdom.

"Let's make some tea, go through pictures, and make tonight about Coty." She looks up to me from my chest. "We'll make it about the both of you rather than the awful stuff that's going on."

I kiss the top of her head and squeeze her gently. "You're seriously amazing."

We reach the house wet, itchy, and covered in clinging vegetation. Damp clothing falls to the floor at the back door in the kitchen and we make our way in our underwear to the living room.

She waits cross-legged on the floor while I retrieve the albums. Coty's baby-book isn't some masterpiece one would share on Pinterest. I took it upon myself to print the countless photos from my phone and computer once Renee left us. They're all collected in a peculiar photo album that looks nothing like an album that should house baby or child pictures.

I find the scrapbook, and several others, in the coat closet near the living room entrance of my home. Several loose pictures are scattered within the wooden Coca-Cola crate the albums reside in. It's obvious the investigators rummaged here as well.

The entire crate is brought out. I figure I can organize as well.

Anguish might be described as a thirty-year-old man sitting among dozens of printed memories, crisp smiles and vibrant life at his fingertips, knowing there will be no more to come—knowing her laughter flooded the same room he now sits in only days prior.

I collect each of the stray photographs from the bottom of the crate while Ashlyn thumbs through the pages that have pictures intact.

The back of my tongue sweats—I'm instantly nauseated as I scan over a picture of Jakabie and Coty on the porch putting puzzles together. One of their favorite pastimes was to take two, one-thousand-piece puzzles and dump them together in the same box. They'd shake it vigorously and then go to work, sorting it all out. Sometimes it would take them the entire day, but the puzzles always ended up in the appropriate boxes.

"Was she a good baby?"

"The best."

Ashlyn's eyes twinkle while looking at the newborn section of Coty's book. She's smitten by my daughter in infant form, and all she has is the pictures to look at.

When we brought Coty home, Renee struggled to find interest in her. Basic needs like feeding and changing our daughter were overwhelming for Renee and I didn't feel comfortable leaving Renee to tend to her alone. Ms. Gonzalez was hired, originally as an in-house nine-to-five nanny, and eventually a babysitter.

I've always struggled with the human psychology and it really shouldn't surprise me why that's so. A woman staring at baby pictures can muster more maternal instinct for my infant daughter than my wife could at the time. Then there's me. I married this woman who carried Coty, birthed her, and wandered away. I befriended a monster shortly after. I welcomed him through my front door, seated him at my dinner table, and showed him to my daughter's bedroom. It's clear there's something to say of my head in those psychology books as well.

"What was her favorite baby food? It looks like she loved carrots…or what the hell ever this stuff is."

Coty is covered in sweet potatoes in a silly picture—one of my favorites. "Ha! Yams. I love that picture. I remember that night. I do believe that was the same night that Biggles showed up, meowing and eating June bugs from our door screen."

"Ew. June bugs?'

"Yes. He loves them."

"On that note, I believe I'll make us some tea."

Pages are skimmed slowly. A lifetime of pictures means so much more when the life is only five years long.

The kettle screams from the kitchen and a few moments later, Ashlyn is setting a piping-hot cup of tea at my side.

"What's this?" She points to a picture of a man with an owl perched on his arm.

I giggle. "Oh, her fourth birthday. It was just a hoot."

"A what?"

"On her fourth birthday, Coty wanted to pet an owl. She's always been fascinated by the ones that nest in the barn. I finally found a rehabber who was willing to travel from Amarillo to here so she could pet her owl."

"Whaaaa…"

"Oh yeah. So, he gets here, and after I pay him a ridiculous amount of money and cash for gas, Coty is horrified by this owl because it looks nothing like the ones in the barn. It's 'big and ugly.' Not to mention, the damn thing shit all over our porch."

Ashlyn chuckles, her hand covering her mouth. "Wow. Do you have any other pictures of the owl? Close-ups?"

"I do. In the back of…" Coty's fifth birthday was well documented; however, those pictures have yet to be added to the album. I flip to the back of the book and tap the great-horned owl for Ashlyn as if she can't see the spooky eyes staring her down from behind the cellophane.

"Ohhh. He's beautiful. He's not ugly at all." She looks closer. "Who is that with Coty and Jakabie?"

I squint. "Oh, that's the Mathews' niece, Lilybeth. She was here from Pueblo so…" as if I've been gut-punched and rendered incapable of speech, I stare at the picture and recall that day.

"What is it, Drake?"

I tap the picture with my index finger. "Lilybeth."

She sucks her bottom lip in for a moment. "Yeah, I didn't think about that. That poor little girl. Maybe you should contact her parents."

"Ashlyn," I tap the picture again, "the day of the party we had purple Kool-Aid for Jakabie. Coty dumped half a glass on this little girl."

Ashlyn's nodding her head, yet she doesn't understand where I'm going with this.

"After her Aunt Maurine washed her off in the

bathroom, she borrowed some of Coty's clothes…the same clothes in this picture."

"Oh. Oh my gosh. A Doc McStuffin's t-shirt."

"And those green shorts. That's where Jakabie got the clothes from." My eyes are widening involuntarily, yet I'm unsure if this means anything significant.

"So, he didn't take them from here, Drake."

"No, he didn't." I stand, blinking and reexamining the factors to see if there's any just cause for hope.

"But that doesn't mean he didn't keep them for trophies."

She's always beautiful, but just now her words are ugly. Every smile I've smiled since Ashlyn called me that morning screeching into the phone that my daughter was gone—every smile has been a Band-Aid smile hiding my gaping wound. Just now I've found something that makes me think maybe…just maybe, my daughter wasn't touched or hurt like that before she was tossed away. And that's yanked away from me within ten seconds of me possessing it.

"I guess here's to wishful fucking thinking." I walk from memory lane to somewhere less volatile, the porch. It's a strange contrast—a cold rocking chair on my bare legs and back and warm air blowing over the front of me.

Biggles joins me at my side. His cool nose presses into the side of my thigh, prompting me to pet him. I oblige.

The whining screen door opening slowly produces a bashful-looking Ashlyn exiting the house. Her eyes, the way she glances at me to ensure it's okay to approach…I feel like a complete asshole.

"Come here." I hold my arm up. "I'm sorry."

"Me too." She positions herself comfortably on my lap. "I only meant…I didn't mean to upset you."

"I know. And you're right. It doesn't matter. Who cares how he got her clothes? He kidnapped her. That's the big picture. Now I just have to focus on what comes tomorrow and how I'm going to deal with that."

"You won't be alone, Drake. Whatever news comes rolling down that dirt road will be handled with me by your side. And when they find that sonofabitch, I'll be right here with you too. I told you, Drake Graves, I'm not going anywhere unless you ask me to."

I wrap my arms around her, pulling her into me. "And I told you, I couldn't do this without you. You are all I have left, Ashlyn."

She kisses my forehead and stands. "Let's go finish our tea and clean up inside."

In the living room, I tuck the albums into the crate as I finish my cooling tea quickly.

Coty's album is the last one. I hold it up, kissing it before setting it in the crate.

"Do you think she can hear you?" Ashlyn asks from behind me.

"What?"

"Do you think Coty can hear you? Do you believe in any of that?"

I shrug. "I don't know. My parents went to church off and on. I never really did. I guess I never had a reason to believe."

A single tear leaves Ashlyn's eye. "At night, I talk to my mother. I tell her how proud she made me. I tell her that I miss her more every day and I'm certain that one day I'll see her face." Her voice is strained as if the words ache leaving her mouth. "I didn't believe either until I had reason to."

My eyes glisten. "What…I don't…I don't know what to say."

"It's okay. Just tuck her in."

I set the crate down, selecting a solitary picture from her birthday in June. She's looking right at me.

"Now's the time to close your eyes, chase your dreams like fireflies. Perhaps tonight, you'll sail the seas, or play patty cake with chimpanzees. A pirate? A princess or even maybe, the caretaker of dragon babies. Some are silly, some are sad. Dreams are dreams, good or bad. But rest assured, some come true. Come morning…come…" I look to Ashlyn as I lose my voice to emotion. Her embrace comes instantly.

"This will always hurt, sugar-bear…but I'm not going anywhere. I'm right here…I'm right here."

# Part II: Ashlyn

# Chapter Eight

I'm in a dangerous place right now. His soft, warm breath on my shoulder is the only sound in the morning lit room. I lie next to him while he sleeps, yet I'm alone with my thoughts. Drake's face, flawless and cradled by soft, white pillows, holds zero resemblance to my father's face. There's nothing about the man next to me that's remotely similar to my dad and yet, I can't seem to shake the thought of my father right now.

As a child, my daddy was a ghost the majority of the year. When Mother would mention him or if he was brought up organically, we would speak of him as though he'd passed on.

He'd show up once or twice a year with gifts and a bottle for himself. In junior high, I realized this was abnormal.

My father left a bar in Cactus, Texas, around three o'clock on a Wednesday afternoon in November 2004.

Witnesses of his death stated he rolled the vehicle multiple times, end over end, and although the majority of his body was ejected from the vehicle, his legs were not. The same witnesses reported he died crying. News of this brought my mother great joy. This too is abnormal.

*What might have been?* Rustling and a deep sigh turn my attention to Drake. Growing up, had I had a fraction of the loyalty and devotion from my own father…oh, the possibilities.

I kiss his scruffy face and slide from beneath the thin white sheet we share. Tiptoeing is pointless, so I slide across the floor in my socks and out the door.

Coffee prepared, I make my way to the porch and inhale the morning air. Today is the day…*everything changes today.*

Reflecting is pointless. I couldn't have imagined when I met Drake that this would be how things played out.

Stepping from the porch and into the yard, the wet, plush grass dampens my socks. Nothing stirs around me; the air is completely still and the only clouds in the sky appear to be happy clouds. By most standards, it would seem to be a good morning. *Most standards.*

Thoughts of family, dead and otherwise, have my brother's voice heavy on my mind. His words buzzing around my ears like relentless black flies, aching to enter and infect my head with his bullshit. But I am thankful to be seeing him soon. Is he truly worthless? All in good time.

Bacon, eggs…possibly some biscuits, depending on how hungry sleepy-boy is. I doubt his nerves allow him to take in much. Last night was a rough one. I'm assuming reckless decisions and grief go hand-in-hand…I wouldn't know.

*Who is calling me?*

Only two people call my phone using a blocked number, and neither of them should be calling me now…it's too early. Adrenaline pumping, I glance toward the door for Drake before darting around the side of the home. The cat, Biggles, happily trots along the house from the opposing direction, blocking my path. I punt him in the face with enough force to sting the top of my foot, sending the stunned sonofabitch spitting and running in the direction he came from.

"Hello?" I angrily answer.

*"Ashlyn?"*

"Who is this?" Low and livid, I press the mouthpiece to my lips, waiting for the woman's response.

*"Sherri, who else would it be?"*

Fire courses through me. A death-grip on my phone has my hand aching as I attempt to calm my rage. "You…stupid *fucking* idiot. What the fuck are you thinking, calling me on my personal phone before it's time?"

*"Oh, my…I certainly hope you didn't use that language around my granddaughter. Absolutely atrocious."*

"Sherri! What the hell?"

*"Ashlyn dear, you tell me."*

"What?"

*"We're rightfully concerned, Ashlyn. This wasn't supposed to be this way."*

"This way? Stand down, drama queen. Is she national news yet? Nah. There's not even a goddamned

GoFundMe account set up. I think we're okay."

*"Ashlyn...why did you take her so soon? It was supposed to be—"*

"Don't patronize me, Sherri. I saw an opportunity and took it. And it's been to our advantage."

There's a slight pause. I peer to either side of me for onlookers, as if I'm smoking a joint outside the gymnasium after the basketball game in high school.

*"Yes...please explain the present situation, if you don't mind, dear."*

"That special needs kid up the road, crazy as hell, his dumbass took off the same night this went down. He's basically been our scapegoat."

*"Scapegoat?"*

"Is there an echo in my phone? Listen, bitch. You're paying me for a service. Everything that we have done...everything that has gone into this is dependent on us following the rules. We do not contact each other until it's done. He'll be there tonight."

*"Ashlyn,"* her voice is surprisingly cold and intimidating, *"you broke the rules first by deviating starkly from the plan. We wouldn't be talking had you not."*

"I told you, I saw an easy win and we took it. Big deal. He'll be there tonight. *Do not* contact me again until it's done and the money has been transferred. I have no clue who's watching, what they know, or how long I really have until they're on to me. Don't call again, bitch."

Rattled by my pulse, my eyeballs dance within my sockets as I stare toward the sky. *Dammit.* And now, I'm left to break the rules as well. I have to call my brother, or I'll spend the entire day on edge, wondering if the plan is on track.

I scroll through my contacts until I find Carter's pimpled face smiling back at me. I press call and almost instantly: *It's Carter. Leave a message.*

At least he follows the rules.

*"En donde estas pinche pendejo? Hablame lo mas pronto que puedas cuando dejes a esa puta. Sherri me hablo preocupada pero le dije a esa puta que se callara. Ahora es la noche hermano."*

Five minutes of pacing and cursing and my nerves are at last calm. Hopefully, I can return to character long enough to keep Drake distracted until tonight.

Up the steps and into the kitchen, I locate a skillet and a pan before cracking the bedroom door to see Drake is still sleeping.

In the kitchen, I prepare him a king's breakfast of fried eggs, biscuits and gravy, and thick bacon. It takes me nearly forty-five minutes to cook this monstrous meal before I fetch him.

I find him on his back in bed, staring at the ceiling. He's expressionless, as if he's a still painting or a photograph.

He remains stoic as I sit next to him on the bed, taking his hand. "Good morning, handsome man."

"Hey." He doesn't look at me when he talks but continues staring toward the ceiling.

Completely flaccid, I bring his hand to my lips, kissing it.

"I cooked for you. Whenever you're ready."

"Thank…thank you." Not even eight in the morning, and already his voice is shaking and his face is tear-streaked…*this is going to be a great day.*

"Would you like milk or orange juice?"

His bottom lip quivers as I wait for a response, and still, no eye contact.

"Drake, your belly growled all night. We need to get something in there." I lean over, kissing his stomach on the area between his belly-button and the waistband of his boxers. His muscles clench.

"Yeah. I'll eat…I'll try to eat in a little bit. I just…I just really miss her. I'm missing her so much right now."

*So selfish. So. Fucking. Selfish.* If it wasn't over tonight…I don't think I could stomach this another day. I wouldn't be surprised if his parents intentionally killed themselves just to be rid of his constant whining. It's unbearable. "It's okay, sugar-bear. You take all the time you need. You know I'm here. Can I get you some water?"

"Please."

I fill his glass, half empty, of course, regardless of how full it is. Slow breaths in, and passive exhalations. *I can do this.* The hard work is over. *I did it.* Excitement has my chest fluttering. Just a few more hours.

In his room, he sips his water. I rub and kiss his back while he remains silent. "Drake, I'm worried about you. Can I make you a plate?"

He takes my hand. "Thank you for cooking, Ash. I'm just…do you mind putting it in the fridge and I'll have it for lunch? I think I'm going to go back to sleep for a while. I'm still tired."

"No. Not at all. Sleep as long as you like. If anyone shows up I'll be here, so no worries."

His head rests into the pillow I've fluffed for him. I stand and shake the sheet before covering him and kissing his cheek.

"Thank you, Ashlyn." Again, with the emotions.

"Of course. Rest. I'm here."

I'm smiling the instant the door closes behind me.

Growing up I never understood the expression, 'Like the day before Christmas.' At school, I'd shy away when conversations and questions regarding Christmas and birthday gifts would arise from friends. It's not that she despised the idea of the holidays, but presents were Daddy's thing, and Momma had enough to worry about in providing food and ensuring the electricity stayed on. But now, at twenty-six years old, I finally mutter to myself… "It's like the day before Christmas."

A tenacious appetite for things other than dilapidated trailer homes put me through nursing school. Ever the opportunist, Momma taught her children to seek out and obtain the fruits of the world. The world is a garden, ripe for the picking.

Her finesse and masterful craft might have landed her somewhere calmer…somewhere with parrots and blue water, had it not been for Dad.

A tequila-soaked plague disguised as a reasonably attractive, rapidly aging Hispanic gentleman…my dad. Corona, Cuervo, cocaine, and panocha…all things my father adored—he'd fall to his knees to lap any of the said four from the shitty, busted tile of the men's restroom at any sleazy establishment, given the chance.

My *gringa* mother, Carter, and I were all things my father resorted to when baggies and bill stacks went low. Looking for a soft place to come down, he'd tap out his signature knock on a flimsy front door. And again, our lives were disrupted for at least a few days. Once Daddy remembered his soft place was shared with roaches, he'd curse Momma, leave a few bruises and holes in the walls, and slam the door on his way out.

No, Drake is nothing like Daddy. Drake is soft and as senseless to the world's cruelty as the lambs he tends. His misery isn't my goal. If it were a possibility to let the boy keep his smile while I find mine, sure— *why not*? But the world doesn't work that way. The world is cold outside, regardless of what the weatherman says in August.

I once envied an odd moth. It had settled on a rotting mattress in our front yard when I was maybe six or seven. White with black trimmed wings and bits of yellow, I thought perhaps it was toxic like the little rainforest frogs we'd learned of in school, so I poked at it with a blade of grass. Eventually, my harassment drove the tiny creature skyward. He left me sitting under a large oak and wondering why I couldn't do the same. Why couldn't I just leave, and *be* somewhere else?

I started running that day. Little laps around the outside of the trailer home, and eventually the entire trailer park. To fly would never be an option but to run, to be swift, with the ability to escape…that's a tool. Momma always talked about acquiring tools of survival.

The trailer park was up in a tizzy when the neighbor's chow-chow…Brutus, I think…was found bound and set ablaze. Carter never admitted to it, but I know he killed that damn dog because it scared me more than anything when I ran…even more than Daddy.

Shit. I said that it was useless to reflect. The point

is…today I'm that moth. *What an accomplishment.* This rotting mattress of a life below me will be a distant memory and I'll have achieved one of my largest goals. A toxic, beautiful little moth, indeed.

"Who the hell is this?" A white sedan with impenetrably black windows has disrupted my nostalgia. Our plan has had well over a year of preparation and has been well-funded, yet each time I see one of these nosy-ass officers tearing down the road, it elevates my heart rate until the imbecile explains what it is they want. This car is different. It's not the blue squad car Officer Salizar drives. I'm both relieved and anxious about this.

Much to my dismay, when the vehicle comes to a stop in the drive, both Salizar and some other man exit. Smiling as they step from the vehicles, my gaze captures only disposable coffee cups…nothing resembling a warrant. Averted. This is the reason Momma hated men and women of the badge. They completely disregard the effort on the opposite end of the spectrum—*numbers behind bars, statistics.*

Their casual approach has me guessing they're here to tell Drake the shit pond search has yielded nothing. *Surprise, surprise.* Still, her over-bleached smile coming up the steps to fuck my morning has me wanting to break her teeth in with the skillet on the stove. I hate her as I open the door.

"Hello? Officer Salizar…is everything okay?" My voice, laced with just enough panic to ensure I'm concerned…to sell it without being overly dramatic. God knows we'll have enough drama when Drake gets his lazy ass out of bed. My eyes, my breath, on the cusp of collapsing—hinging on their words. I assure my glance is equally shared between the two of them.

"Ashlyn, sweetheart, this is Special Agent Alvarado. Is Drake home?"

Swallowing hard, I step aside. "He's in bed still. He's not…he's just not doing well today." My voice cracks—hand to my mouth as a single tear falls. It's stunningly perfect.

"Oh?" Salizar's hand is on my shoulder.

"No. I can't get him to eat. I'm so worried. He's just…fading."

The officers make their way through the kitchen, Alvarado following Salizar like an ugly puppy to the drowning pond.

I watch and listen as they make their way into the room without even knocking. *Typical pigs*. Their voices carry through the home. I hear something resembling encouragement in Drake's voice as they mention the likelihood of the call being placed by a disgruntled former employee.

Drake is stumbling through the door; the officers are behind him as they talk and he listens excitedly. Wide and wild, his eyes devour each word their mouths mumble. It's deplorable.

Dumbfounded in his boxer shorts, he scratches his balls while sporting a half smile. *These idiots*.

It's a thing of beauty and balance. Rather than provide Drake a powerboat as he chokes and gasps in a river of grief, I've tossed him a petite raft. Then, I poked a hole in it—leaving his head just above the rapids.

There is nothing more annoying than a weak and sniveling man, crying like a bitch for days. But, giving him too much confidence means giving him the motivation to explore and investigate, and there's already enough of that going on as it is.

"Did you hear that, Ash?" His arms wide as he walks to me—unbathed, and open for a hug. "They're almost certain it was a false tip…a disgruntled caller."

"Yay!" I hug him. It truly isn't that I'm displeased by his happiness. Drake is a sweet guy, and if I were driving down the road with the option of swerving or hitting him for fun, I would more than likely spare him.

"So, wait." Peeking over Drake's shoulder, I lock eyes with Salizar. "A prank caller? Seriously?"

She nods. "We're finding no reason to believe otherwise."

"Okay," I push off of Drake, "but what about Drake? He's been tortured by this. Whoever this disgruntled person is, they need to be held accountable."

"Trust me, miss, we're looking into it." The bastard, Alvarado, responds. His tone, the way his stare narrows has me sinking within myself. There's no way they know I placed that call. The phone I called from was a black market prepaid Mexican gadget from a trashy vendor in Guymon. "Well…I hope you find that woman. She's deplorable."

"It is in our interest to find her," Alvarado continues.

"It smells lovely in here…like hickory-smoked bacon." Salizar's snout sniffs at the air like a swine being slopped.

"Yes!" I clap my hands together. "Please tell me you two officers haven't had breakfast yet. I can't get this man to eat and I'd hate to see that mountain of food go to waste." I pat Drake's four-pack abs from the side as I wait for the pigs to respond.

"Actually, Ashlyn, I'm a little hungry." Drake

happily proclaims as he stretches.

"That's what I like to hear. You go get some clothes on before the early birds see the worm…and I'll heat up the stove." He chuckles as I kiss his cheek and send him to his room.

Salizar and Alvarado sit silently at the bistro table. I feel Alvarado's eyes on me—his fat head turning with me as I meander through the kitchen. "More coffee, anyone?"

"I'll take a warm-up." Alvarado the atrocity raises his cup. The back of his head is even fatter—as if someone has stapled three rows of horizontal hotdogs along the posterior of his cranium.

"I'm thankful he's going to eat. I can't seem to get anything down him."

"Ashlyn." Salizar's hand rests on my arm as I pour coffee. "This isn't cause for false hope. It merely means she isn't there, which is a good thing."

*A good thing?* You've prematurely demolished my diversion. *This is a horrible thing.* "Last night, I held him in the living room while he wept. The idea of his beautiful daughter being disposed of like that…this is a cause for hope. I'm so thankful you all are at least able to give him that."

Salizar nods in agreement.

"I'm assuming you two like bacon?" *Pigs!*

Resounding yesses have me placing several greasy pieces on their plates along with eggs and biscuits. As I serve them, Drake walks in. Gym shorts and a white t-shirt…and a smile. At least I won't have to be his Kleenex again today.

"Hungry, bubba?"

"A little."

The porcelain plate is loaded heavily with eggs and bacon, and of course, love. *It's all for the prize.*

The officers are gone within the hour, promising to return should anything transpire.

So much is to be done and yet there isn't. Much like the moth I once envied, my departure will be simple and will hopefully go mostly unnoticed.

Packed, ready, and aching for me to grab it and go, my bag and life are waiting for me just inside the front door of my house. This instant I get that call tonight…I'm gone.

"Ashlyn." I ease into his cradling body as he pulls me into him from behind.

"My hands are covered in dish soap, crazy kid." Facial whiskers trace the nape of my neck and hot breath has me biting my bottom lip, contemplating turning to him and ripping his shorts around his ankles. Primal and satisfying, Drake's ability to send my eyes rolling to the back of my skull is a feat I'll acknowledge any day. A soft bitch when the clothes are on, but as soon as I've got that man in my bed…he does make the transition from pussy to tiger.

Wet and sudsy, my hand slides between his legs to find he's as soft as hot bubble gum. I literally can't tell cock from balls in my grasp.

"What the hell, Ash?" He bucks his butt backward, yanking his junk from me as I turn to him.

*Eh. Puke.* He wasn't coming onto me. The dude's all teary-eyed, *again!* And wiping his face on me like a goddamned snot rag. I can't do this…yes, I can. *You can do this, Ashlyn.* "I'm sorry, sugar-bear. I…I couldn't find a dish-towel. I wasn't reaching for your goodies. Did I hurt you?"

"No," he whimpers, taking me in a hug. Okay, maybe if given the chance, I *would* run him over in the road. Yes, I would…*definitely.*

"This is just so crazy, you know?"

"Come again?" I kiss his neck.

"She's not there in that lagoon. I'm just so relieved of that."

I take his hand in mine. "I know. And look how much time those incompetent officers wasted looking there…and over an anonymous tip. Amateurs."

He scowls and smiles at the same time. "I highly doubt they've concentrated all their efforts there. Especially for a single, anonymous tip. They know more than they're telling us."

His words, and the confidence within them have me flustered. He's right. This isn't surprising. We anticipated we'd have a small window of opportunity. *Tonight…it ends tonight.*

My brain is abuzz as the afternoon sifts by like watching a sundial. I'm dying to know if Carter killed Jakabie. If he did, it's flipping genius, but it went against the plan—broke the rules. And if he didn't, Jakabie is just out there, waiting to be found like a Special-Olympics wild card, itching to screw me over by collapsing the psycho-next-door theory, just before I make my great escape.

Hope. It's in the way he walks through the home. The octave of his voice is a tad lower, less distressed today. As we enter the evening hours, it's apparent that Drake has found hope within the fact that little Coty isn't bobbing in pig shit stew like a giant corn kernel. He may not admit it, but he feels she may be living…I can sense it. This would be a potential problem *if* this wasn't my last evening dealing with the bullshit. Hope blooms miracles, and I'm sure a desperate daddy's broken heart is the perfect place to plant that shit. Not for you, bubba. Sorry, *sugar-bear*.

"Drake."

"Yeah, babe?"

"I'm going to run into town. I need to run by the hospital, check my schedule, and grab some clothes. What would you like to eat?"

He stands, smiling. "Can I come with you?"

Dammit! *Damn you!* "Sure, sugar-bear. What sounds good for supper?"

And his gaze shifts instantly to the ceiling. Every time I ask him what he wants to eat he looks to the ceiling like there's a goddamned menu painted up there.

"Hmmm. Maybe some jalapeno cheese balls and a burger?"

*Puke*. "That sounds delicious. We'll make that two. We should call the order in now so it's ready when we get there."

He looks to me. "What if…what if Salizar comes back out? What if they find something and I'm not here?"

*So stupid. They're not going to find anything.* "Make you a deal, I'll skip the hospital. I'll just grab some clothes, grab our supper, and I'll be back in no time."

"No time, huh? Sounds good. I think it's about time I hit the shower anyway. It's not fair to continue subjecting you to this."

His grin is always disarming. There's some small nudging inside me…something that may resemble heartache but on a lesser level. When these strange revelations occur, I attempt to embrace them, as I find they make me somewhat more human. Legitimate emotion—no acting, has me looking at Drake, mildly saddened I'll never be in his company again. *Fuck it.* "I'll be right back, bubba. I love you."

His arms around my waist, lifting me up off of the ground, he kisses my grinning lips. "I love you more. So much more."

*Yes, you do, Drake Graves...yes, you do.* "Not possible."

# Chapter Nine

Even at its busiest, Main Street is passive. Yet, today I feel their eyes on me. Beady, judgmental, and gawking awkwardly as I drive by—faces plastered in a faux sympathy.

Greasy and aromatic, the food order that will never be consumed is sitting in my passenger seat. When Drake's calls go unanswered, he'll undoubtedly call the establishment to see if I've been there to pick up the food—*track coverage*. In my driveway and free from the gazes of busy people with nothing to do, I fill my lungs and hold it several seconds. This is it. Freedom with a phone call.

In my home, pacing like a caged lioness, I await the keys to my new life.

"Dammit…come on."

Just as my anxiety has peaked, my phone vibrates within my hand. The words, Unknown Caller…*beautiful*.

Excitedly pushing the phone to my face, I squat to the bag by the door, ready to fly from my home and this tired scene. "Hello?"

*"Ashlyn?"* Sherri's monotone voice enters my ear.
"Yes? Sherri?"

*"Where are they? Where is my granddaughter?"*

Upright and wide-eyed, I drop my bag. "There…Carter is there. That's the plan! Don't fuck with me."

*"Ashlyn! Listen to what I am saying! The area has been scouted and our people have been there for well over an hour. DeCota and your brother are not there!"*

"No…oh my god, no. This isn't happening." My mind is mush-like. Too many scenarios are colliding at once.

*"Listen to me, Ashlyn. Do you hear me now?"*

"Yes. I'll figure this—"

*"If my granddaughter has been harmed in any way…any way…there will be no hiding for half-bred scum like you and your brother."*

Anger joins the mixture of emotions swirling within me. "Did you really just go there, you dried up old cunt?"

*"Ashlyn."*

"Carter will be there with your snot-nosed brat. There has to be an explanation for this. Call me back in one hour."

I'm calling my brother the instant I press end on the conversation with Sherri. Again, it goes directly to voicemail. Like the little girl jumping over old car parts and dashing down the dirt drive toward my home in the trailer park with a ravenous Brutus on my heels…I am horrified. This is emotion. This is raw and genuine and human and I ache to give it back. I want the life I've worked for. The life etched in my mind when my eyes close.

Be it breaking my Uncle Richie's knuckles for drinking too much and climbing in bed with me, or filling the neighborhood with the agony of Brutus—bound and burning while his owner was helpless to save him, Carter has always protected me. Protection with a price. It was small things while we were children. My mother would praise my ability to con the school secretary when she broke ten-dollar bills for me. I'd walk to class with four one-dollar bills, two fives, and a buck in quarters.

The beauty in my craft evaded Carter. Rather than enchant and allure, he's one to move in and brutally acquire. To each their own, but he often recruited me—or enlisted, rather.

I'd be bullied into breaking into the school and stealing the entire cash box rather than swindling Ms. Trish out of a few extra bucks. Or waiting until an alley-parked truck driver was well inside of a store, but after the dumbass had left his trailer open…we'd cash in on Cheetos, DVD players, and one time a driver left his daughter's band camp fundraising money in the console. Two hundred eighty dollars. We lived high that summer.

This is different. I'm an idiot to have believed Carter wouldn't hold Coty for additional ransom after the kidnapping. That is exactly what happened. *It has to be!*

"That fucker!" This is unamendable. There's no reasoning with psychopathy and the bastard won't even answer his phone. *How could he?* I did the real work.

I worked at the clinic across the street from the hospital when Renee brought Coty in for her checkups. Renee is batshit crazy, but she's the kind of crazy you can't do anything with—it's useless. It's apparent in her eyes, just below the surface, she's like a wild fucking animal, but one that needs to be continuously medicated. The day she approached me, popping off about a background check and me being the perfect fit…I thought she'd lost her mind. It wasn't until the conversation with Sherri and the mention of seven digits that I took heed to what was being offered.

We have spent well over a year in preparation for this, just waiting for the green light from the north to make our move. And now I'm discredited. I'll kill him. I'm going to kill Carter when I find him.

Pacing once more, I feel mildly nauseated each time I glance toward the packed bag in the floor. I should be driving south by now. I should be Juarez-bound.

The hour oozes by and finally, my phone is vibrating again.

"Hello? Sherri?"

*"Anything, Ashlyn? Have you heard from Carter?"*

My magnum opus of a scam seeps from the canvas right before me…leaves me blank and staring at my laced shoes—all tied and nowhere to run.

*"No. Sherri, listen to what I'm about to tell you. I know my brother. I think he'll ask for ransom."*

There's a low chuckle in the phone. *"Dear. A great deal of this year has been spent on preparation, has it not?"*

I clear my throat. "Yes."

*"Alternate identities…a new residence for my family…a chance to do this right, as we failed miserably with Renee. So much preparation…don't you think it might have behooved us to have had a plan B?"*

"What…what do you mean?"

*"A plan B, dear. This is so much more than a simple abduction. This a new chapter in several beautifully constructed novels. Do you truly think I'd be so ignorant as to hand the pen to the likes of you without insurance?"*

This bitch is making no sense to me. "Listen to me…I will find your granddaughter and you will have her as we agreed upon. I promise you that."

*"And you listen to me, Ashlyn. It would be wise if you made good on that promise sooner rather than later. I hired you, not because I was short on options, but because I felt a simple, efficient job with a capable, intelligent local was possible. I know many people with many skillsets…find my granddaughter."*

"Wha…are you threatening…hello? Sherri?" There's no one there.

Another attempt to reach Carter and still nothing. Just as my phone is sliding into my pocket—vibration. *Could it be?*

Drake. His name stares at me from my screen and I realize I'm in limbo. I can't ignore him.

"Hey, sugar-bear."

*"Hey, gorgeous. It's…it's been a minute. I'm a little hungry."*

I'm dying inside right now…my life, all I've worked for is being savagely yanked from me and I'm defenseless to stop it, and he's 'a little hungry?' How self-absorbed can he be? "I'm sorry, bubba. I'm coming to you right now."

*"You okay, Ash?"*

Raw…real… "Nope."

*"Talk to me, beautiful. I'm here for you, too."*

I sigh. "Just…just stuff with Coty." *Totally truthful.*

*"I know. This is hard on you, I know it is. I'll run you a bath tonight and rub your back. Sound good?"*

I wish he'd take a bath while blow drying his pretty-boy hair. "Sounds amazing. I love you, Drake."

My fist pummels the center of the steering wheel at random during the drive to Drake's house. The shift in mindset is so disheartening. My lottery ticket…scratch that, my payday, has been ripped away from me and I'm left stunned and clueless.

The drive to his house has always had a purpose before. As he comes into view on the front porch, rocking in his chair like he's ninety, I realize every drive down this road may have been for nothing.

Open arms welcome me to failure as I exit the vehicle and ascend the porch steps. Smiling back is the worst.

Crouched and fearful, Biggles cowers beneath Drake's rocking chair. He scans my every move for a second or two and then slinks away.

Drake takes me in his arms, pulling me into his chest. He smells clean like sheets fresh from the dryer…yet there's nothing comforting here. His embrace is restraining. A moth without wings, I'm left to wander about the gravel and bake in the sun and the consequences of my actions.

"That food need to be heated up?" He kisses my cheek.

The bag of burgers, and other greasy delights, was residing in my trash until just prior to my return. "You might nuke it a second or two, sugar-bear."

In the kitchen, I watch him eat casually, as if both our skies aren't fractured above us…one wrong move could bring them crashing down.

"You look beautiful tonight." His boyish grin, the way he talks with a bite in his mouth…if only I had a shotgun.

"Thank you." I stare at the burger while it stares at me. "I'm not feeling so well. I think I'm going to sit this one out. I'll put this bad-boy in the fridge and you can have it for lunch tomorrow."

"Okay. I'll go run you a bath—"

"I think I just want to throw on a t-shirt and sleep. Is that okay?"

He nods. His eyes course with concern, yet I can't find it within me to display anything but what I feel now. Defeated and depleted. I kiss his face and make my way to the room, checking my phone one last time. Carter's voicemail message enters my ear once more as I slip beneath the sheets.

An odd thing happens. My eyes burn and flood without being prompted. *This is real*. This is emotion.

Curling up, I turn to see Drake enter the room. He slips in next to me.

"I'm sorry, baby-doll. Talk to me."

I wipe my eyes. "It's just Coty. We don't know where she is. And I can't get a hold of my brother. I've never needed him more in my life and he's abandoned me. He's left me."

Soft lips to my forehead, and then Drake is rubbing my head. I'm leaving the day behind. Tomorrow I'll have Sherri, the investigators, and the world to deal with. Tonight, I rest with my prey.

Soft knocking enters my ears. I open my eyes to find I'm in bed alone. The night has left me dreamless. Conversation is coming from the kitchen—a woman's voice and Drake. Morning is all around me like some sickness I can't escape. Birds chirping just outside and the alarm clock stares me down with a glaring red 08:04.

After adding a pair of shorts to my attire, I make my way to the kitchen to find Drake and some haggard-looking Hispanic woman at the table. A mound of Kleenex is crumpled before either of them on the bistro when I walk in. They weep and smile at the same time the way pathetic people do when they're trying to remember the good times, but they're sad about it.

"Ash. This is Ms. Gonzalez. She meant the world to Coty. Coty loved her very much."

Ms. Gonzalez is a ravishing beauty. Her makeup appears to have been spray painted on and her reddish hair looks as though she found a dead animal on the road several years ago and attempted to style it appropriately. It's difficult to take the woman seriously, staring down at her quivering biscuit lips—painted pink.

"It's a pleasure to meet you, Ms. Gonzalez." I take her weathered hand in mine as she looks curiously at me.

"Excuse me, ladies. I need to run to the restroom." Drake stands, and only now is he offering up his seat. *Typical*.

He disappears as her gaze narrows. "Is…" Her finger shakes. "Is your father Hector Ramirez?"

Smiling, I nod. "Yes. That was his name. Were you familiar?"

"Oh! Si. Si, I was. I'm so sorry to hear. So sorry."

"It's fine."

"Your mother Jane is in Juarez, yes?"

I grin once more. The orphan tale I pushed down

Drake's throat—our commonality, is a key fundamental in our foundation. How does this bitch know my parents? Where the fuck is she from? "I'd rather not speak of my parents, ma'am."

"Oh. Is her health poor—"

"Not now, please."

She overexaggerates her frown before her eyes pierce through me. "Drake told me…he said once he dated an orphan girl. A little orphan, just like him. He laughed about it. I know Jane. I knew Hector, and where you came from."

It's impossible to swallow as I hear Drake walking back to the kitchen across the hardwood. Well, shit. *I guess it can't get any worse.*

"Ms. Gonzalez is making us dinner tonight, Ash," Drake happily proclaims.

"Oh. How sweet of her." My sly smile has Ms. Gonzalez staring at me the way Biggles does when I step from my car.

"Yes. Yes, I will be back this evening. Drake, you call me, or send me a text message on my cellular phone if the plans change?" She stands, pecking him on the cheek.

"Of course, but they won't." He pats his stomach and smiles like an idiot.

I watch her shitty S-10 drive away from the kitchen window and know my time is coming. There are too many loose ends and the world is literally too small.

My parents were some shady people, but the shade they cast was mostly in Texas. How in the hell is it that this woman knows my mother and father? I've never seen her before in my life.

"Drake." I summon his attention.

"Yeah, babe."

"Ms. Gonzalez, what does she know about us? What have you told her?"

He smiles. "Told her? I've only mentioned you a few times."

"And?"

"And what?" He crosses his arms.

"What all have you mentioned?"

"That I was seeing a girl. That I had met a girl and we had a lot in common."

"That's it?"

Drakes chuckles as he walks to me. "Was she giving you a hard time? She's really protective."

"Just tell me, sugar-bear."

"Alberta Gonzalez is one of the sweetest people I've ever known…but she's also the nosiest. I don't really divulge information because she's so overwhelming sometimes. She literally checks to make sure I'm buying the brand of fabric softener and toilet paper she recommends when she visits. She's just…different."

I giggle, but I'm sure I look disgusted.

"Don't be mad I didn't give a lot of details…like your job…or name." He laughs.

"I'm not mad, you goofball. She was just a little intense." I sway with him in my arms.

"Yeah, Coty adored her though. Hey, I think I'm going to run to the clinic and then make a house call today. I think it might clear my head. Wanna go with me?"

I squeeze him around the waist. Sinister conspiracies brew within me. "No. I think I need to make a house run, too. I need to grab some things."

Faded blue jeans and a ball cap and he's out the

door. Finally, I can stretch and walk freely without tripping over that man's twelve-foot tampon string.

Knowing I don't have much time, I search through his card file on his desk.

"Got ya, Ms. Gonzalez."

Hopefully, she lives alone. I highly doubt, given how grotesque she truly is, that she is married or in a relationship. The address shows she lives literally seven minutes away and just as rural as I am now. Perfect.

I'm calm and collected, unlike the dust tearing across my side windows as I drive down the dirt road toward her home. *I'm coming for you, Ms. Gonzalez.* There are too many cinders yearning to burst into flames and set my world ablaze to not extinguish those that I can.

If blood was unremovable, my brother's hands would glow a bright burgundy. Initially, I believed he took lives for logistical purposes. As we grew older, his tales grew more gruesome. The whites of his eyes would burn bright with excitement as he reenacted the scenes of mutilation. No shock. As a child, more than a handful of times, a foul smell would lead me to the disfigured corpse of a stray puppy, kitten, or wild animal within a shoebox under his bed. Mother would chuckle and ramble on about Carter's wild imagination and creativity. He'd choke me out on occasion. I'd lie willingly on my bed, his knees in my chest, his hands around my throat until the dark encompassed and consumed the world I looked upon. But…every time I'd awaken to his sweet smile. He's always been there for me in his own way.

Ms. Gonzalez' shitty S-10 is parked in front of a

trashy, white, 80's-looking trailer house with blue trim. The yard is open and littered with chickens running about it. *What a life.*

Parked behind her, I make my way to the welded metal porch, but the sound of music catches my attention. Following the rectangular home to the back, I find her in an impressive garden, on her knees in the soil. A large woven straw hat shields her monstrous hair. She sings, bouncing her head along happily to her music as I approach casually.

"Hola!"

She shrieks and lands backward in the soil on her fat ass. "Oh! Oh dear. You scared me."

I stand over her. My cast shadow shields her eyes from the sun behind me. "Oh. What a pity."

"What do you want?"

This is a good question. I've never taken a life before. There's nothing about bloodshed that remotely interests me, but I know what I want, and this thing before me is just one more object in the way…an object I might be able to do something about. "Let's go inside. Now."

She stands, dusting herself. "I think it's best if you leave—"

I charge her. She raises her hand in defense, but my open palm slaps her face with a force that sends her hat falling.

*"Oh!"*

I grab her arm, my gaze locked to hers. "Listen, bitch. Do you wanna die out here in the dirt like a dog?" My grip squeezes her flabby arm.

She shakes her head as tears stream.

"Inside!"

The inside of her humble trailer house smells much like many of my childhood homes. A faint hint of pine cleaner and taco seasoning lingers in the walls, carpets, and air.

Her hands are tightly clasped by the sink. She stares at me, her eyes pleading as I search frantically through her medications. There are several Hydrocodone prescriptions but I'm wanting something fast.

My glance skims past an empty box of glucometer lancets. "Are you diabetic?"

"Yes."

I walk to her, touching her shoulder. "Why didn't you tell me?" The refrigerator has four vials of insulin. I grab them all. "Sit."

"Oh!" She wails out. "No. Oh, no, no. Please!" Her pleas remind me of Geppetto when Pinocchio accidentally sets his finger afire. As children, Carter and I watched *Pinocchio* and *Texas Chainsaw Massacre* religiously on VHS. We wore those tapes out.

I reach for a knife as she makes the sign of the cross and mutters something.

"Open casket or closed. Your choice."

She weeps but sits as I draw up the entire first bottle. "Where do you want it, sweetie?"

Her soft cries fill the kitchen as I gently give the first injection. "Wasn't so bad. Next." This continues until her supply is gone and four little bottles sit happily for her to see—transparent executioners, smiling in a row.

Her cries are heavy at first, but quickly weaken as she fans herself. "I'm...oh. I don't want to die."

I nod understandingly. "I get it. But you just couldn't keep your fucking mouth shut."

"Oh…oh please, I don't feel good." Her words slur. Beads of sweat speckle her forehead.

"I know. You're committing suicide." I reach under her arm, lifting her from the chair. "Let's get you to the couch and comfy."

"Please!" Her cries effortlessly fill the small home.

"Hush now. Just lie down here. I'll stay with you until you've passed." I set her down and position her feet on the couch. "Better?"

"W…why? How are you so cruel to me and I've done nothing to you?" Her face is melting into the pillow. She's fading.

"Cruel? Look at you. You're going in style."

Her lips pout, tears stream, and then she sleeps. I grab a blanket to cover her. *God, she's even more hideous unconscious.*

After wiping my prints from the bottles, I place them on her trashy garage-sale coffee table and the syringe in her hand.

Her phone is an old person phone. It has ridiculously large buttons on it and only seven contacts. So cute. Most importantly, it's easily located and I don't need a password to unlock it. A simple text to Drake to cancel dinner plans, and there you have it. My first murder. *So exciting!*

Right now, I should be able to call my brother and brag. He'd act hard, but I know he'd be proud and we'd laugh about the details and meet up for a congratulatory beer later.

Distraction abolished, it's time to focus on bigger issues. I leave the shitty trailer and Ms. Gonzalez lifeless inside.

# Chapter Ten

The kitchen is a quiet place to collect my thoughts when the home is empty. There's something enjoyable about hearing the singing birds and calling pheasants in the fields. Sipping my tea, I find myself grinning in silence and even giggling all alone like a crazy person as I reflect on the events of the afternoon. Silly Alberta. So theatrical and dramatic. Not to mention her face was the stuff of nightmares, but it's the voice that gives me the giggles. It's funny how people will pick out the little things from an equation and cling to them. I'll always remember the first life I took because of her funny little voice. Thank you for that, Alberta Gonzalez.

A truck engine kills my nostalgia. Seconds later, dirty Drake comes through the door of the kitchen. Something about my first kill has me excited, and Drake isn't helping the situation. His scent, his stubble…if only he wouldn't speak.

"That's so odd. I hope she's okay," he says as he opens the fridge for a beer, talking into the phone. "I'm sure she's fine," he continues. "This must be rough on her too."

He closes the fridge, swigging his beer, nodding his head as if whoever he's talking to can see him. *So fucking stupid.*

This douche. The jeans he's rocking basically scream—*he squats*. His Tom Petty t-shirt is dirty from the day and hugs his chest and biceps. His ball cap, face, and boots are dusted in dirt too. If I wasn't mistaken, I'd think I had a man in front of me…a gorgeous one at that. And there's nothing I can do about it. My mind is racked with stress and the number-one stress reliever is glaring at me from just under the worn material of his pants.

"Sounds good." He hangs up the phone and eyes the refrigerator once more. "Dammit if enchiladas didn't sound amazing." His throat throbs with each swig as he chugs his longneck down.

"I'll cook your enchiladas, silly boy." I remove his hat, running my fingers through his hair.

"Really?" His hand rests on the small of my back and pushes me into him.

"Yes. There isn't much I wouldn't do for you."

He swallows hard—his Adam's apple bouncing in his throat. His breath deepens as my fingers trace over his lower belly. "Ash…it just doesn't…it wouldn't feel right."

I giggle. "Sugar-bear, you have been under so much stress. Let me take that away, if only for a few minutes."

He smirks, glancing away. "A few? Just a few minutes?"

*Game on.*

I've heard enough of that goddamned mouth so I shove it to mine, pushing him into the counter.

"Wait," he snivels. "I can't. I can't do this right now."

*Pathetic.* He gently pushes me backward, looking at me like the poster child for Zoloft. I bet half the depressed dudes of the world would be better post-lay from a willing participant. And what about me? I'm all but desperate to get some and all I get is this weakness.

"Oh. Okay." I lean over, kissing his lips. "I understand, bubba. I'm just trying to help you."

This is the second time that little snot-nosed brat, Coty, has interrupted my pleasure, and this time she's not even in the same vicinity.

"Are you upset with me, Drake?"

He shakes his head. "No. No, not at all, Ash. My head is so full of other stuff and this just doesn't feel right." He kisses my nose.

"Okay. So, sugar…would you like chicken or beef enchiladas?"

Drake downs mass quantities of beer in the kitchen. Shirtless and bubbly, I know it's only a matter of time before the alcohol produces the shriveled, sacless tit-bag, bawling and carrying on.

Something dark lurks within me. Some odd resentment has me looking at Drake in a vengeful way. Before, he was merely a casualty of my plot. But now, I want to hurt him. I know he's hurting. The world knows he's hurting because he's constantly crying over something that happened *days* ago, but I want to twist the dagger and I can't.

"Wow. I think maybe I overdid it. You care if I take a little nap?" His belch fills the kitchen as he stands and stretches.

"Not at all, sweetie. Go get you some rest. I'll wake

you when supper is ready."

He smells of sour beer and a day's work outdoors as he wraps his clammy arms around me. "I love you, Ashlyn. Thank you for being so good to me." His words whisk by my ear, angering me further.

"I love you too, Drake. Get some rest."

With Drake resting, I stew in the kitchen. I've heard nothing from Carter or Sherri. As if waiting isn't awful enough, I have to do it with this bumbling asshole with more mother issues than *Hustler Magazine*. The thought of cooking for him has my nails digging into my palms.

Just as my irritation spills over into anger range, I hear the calling of the purrrfect ingredient for enchiladas. Biggles beckons from the front porch, demanding to be fed.

I can't control the devious smile as I open the drawer and find the rolling pin. Initially, Biggles is wary when I exit the door, but he's a fan of the milk I set before him and laps it up at the side of the house, oblivious to my intentions. He gurgles on blood and flops about after the initial blow to the skull. Two more finish him off and I quickly carry him to the barn by the tail. Cleaning him isn't much different than cleaning squirrels and chickens. He smells awful inside, but I'm sure with the right seasoning, he'll make a fine dinner for Drake.

Deboned, cubed, and spiced with exact precision, the scent of fried Biggles fills the home. It's an hour later and my sleepy boy is exiting the bedroom, just as I'm pulling my masterpiece from the oven.

There's nothing more disgusting than morning breath in the evening, especially when it's beer battered. He hugs me from behind, gleefully eyeing the pan of food.

"You've outdone yourself, babe."

"Anything for you, Drake. Grab a seat while this cools."

His eyes eagerly follow me as I set his plate in front of him at the table. He licks his lips and I hand him a fork. "Careful, sugar-bear. It's really hot."

"It smells amazing."

"Daddy's recipe. That man could cook some Mexican food."

I sit across from Drake as the fork takes the first bite to his mouth. He chews. The dagger is twisting and he's clueless of the damage. This is beautiful.

"Is it delicious, Drake?"

He swallows. "Um, it's good. This is chicken?"

"Seasoned to perfection."

He nods, taking another bite.

"Would you like a Tecate to wash that down?"

"Sure."

*Alcoholic!* I hand him his beer, delighting in my work. I'm surrounded by idiocy and uncontrollable circumstances, but this is self-care. This is my way of giving back to him all that he has cast on me. *Fuck him.*

"It's been a quiet day, Drake. Hasn't it?"

He swallows, only nodding as he eyes his plate with a concerned look on his face.

"What's the matter, cat got your tongue?"

"Uh, Salizar called earlier. They should have some results from the labs soon. That's all she said really."

"Oh."

"I'm full. I think this isn't sitting well with the beer."

"No problem. I'll wrap this up for tomorrow if you

like."

I usher my boy to bed with a belly of beer and Biggles. He lies face down on the sheets as I massage his thick shoulders. Soon enough he's snoring and taking up the majority of the mattress. What a life. I imagine the day when all I'm working for is rewarded and I'm not left to play housewife to some douche who won't even put out.

The evening drifts away. Once again, I'm closing my eyes in hell rather than Mexico. Tomorrow. Tomorrow will come with answers.

It's not sand, but I feel dirty. My entire body. Looking to my left, the dark figure is unrecognizable. I want to call for Drake…shout for him, yet my mouth doesn't seem to work. The walls, the ceiling…they're familiar, yet they're not what I looked upon when I closed my eyes. Cheap and temporary, like paper plates, the thin wood-paneling around me is from my bedroom—my childhood bedroom. It's an odd thing, to recognize I'm dreaming and on the cusp of a nightmare, yet there's nothing I can do but breathe. I'd never look to Drake for safety or security, but surely, he can shake me…wake me before it happens. This is emotion. This reoccurrence leaves me twisted in the sheets, gasping and sweating and clinging to my face and hair as I finally emerge from my mind's torture. Why? Why am I here again? Why can't Drake hear me? The figure beside me inches closer, just as I'm able to control my thumb and index finger enough to pinch my thigh. I sit forward, looking upon white walls and a white ceiling. Drake's dumb ass sleeps soundly at my side, oblivious to my plight…to my struggle. Without a second thought, my open palm descends from above, slapping the shit out of his drunken, sleeping face.

"Hey!" He riles, looking about as I slump down and close my eyes. "What the…what the fuck?"

I want to laugh. I am laughing inside and it makes it nearly impossible to keep my eyelids sealed shut. He fluffs his pillow, moves around a bit, and within minutes he's snoring again.

I don't dare drift off again. Not tonight. I know what's waiting for me, just this side of consciousness. I'll wait patiently for morning. It'll give me time to think.

The hours pass surprisingly quick. Pale light pours through the home.

I sit on the edge of the bed, listening to Drake's soft snores. Amazingly, I'm not left wanting to smother him. It's possible that slapping the fuck out of him in the middle of the night had some therapeutic quality to it. Certainly cathartic. I'm mildly content for the time being. *Fuck it.* A small amount of time will be spent prodding around and attempting to learn Carter's next move. Then I'll go. Carter can't live without me, even if he's banked my payday, he needs me too much. Eventually, he'll come slithering.

Drake's phone rings from atop his nightstand. He scurries from the sheets before grabbing it and slapping it to his face.

"Hello?" He clears his throat. "I'm here." Propping up on his elbow with a creased forehead—his expression showcases immense concern.

"What? Slow down. Two?"

His eyes lock on mine. I ache to know what he knows. *Should I be running now?* Are the words driving in his ear all he needs to be provided with to end me?

"I'm here. I'm here right now…yeah. Yeah, we'll be here."

He sets the phone aside, crawling from the bed. "Shit."

"What?"

"That was…um…that was Salizar." He pauses and pinches his bottom lip between his thumb and index finger, staring at the floor.

"Drake, words! What the hell is going on?" I clap my hands—taking us both aback. "Sorry."

"You're fine. Sorry. The lab results—the blood found on Coty's doll and in Jakabie's bedroom. The blood is from two people."

"What?"

He shrugs. "Salizar was rambling."

"Are you going to the station or—"

"She's coming here. She just wanted to make sure I was home…like I'd be anywhere else."

We wait in the kitchen. Caffeine seems to have only exacerbated my racing heart rate.

Chewing the inside of my cheek at the bistro, I jump as his cool hand rests atop mine.

"You okay? You seem jittery."

I shake my head. "Why don't they just move in out here? Or set you up a room at the police station?"

"What?" His eyelids squint. He's lost.

"It's like, every time these idiots have anything new to tell you, they're jumping in their vehicles and racing out here. We have phones for a reason. I'm just done with seeing them."

He looks disgusted—possibly angered. "Um, they're investigating Coty's disappearance. She has more questions and needs to talk with me face to face. I don't see the problem."

My anger is quelled to the best of my ability. "You're right. Sorry."

Finally, Salizar's stupid ass is pulling into the drive. At least this time she left the hot dog head, Alvarado, at home.

She knocks once before barreling through the kitchen door.

"All right, Drake. We have some stuff to discuss." She stands over me, her gaze excusing me from my seat so that she might have it.

I lean into the counter, desperate for the information within the file she carries.

"Okay." She removes papers and a few pictures of Jakabie's room from the file. "The lab has the results from the samples we sent them."

Drake's eyes are wide with anticipation.

"The blood on Coty's stuffed doll matched the samples we obtained from the home and the swabs we obtained from you."

"Shit." Drake bows his head to the table.

"It was trace. A very small amount. Nothing indicative of mass blood loss. However, in Jakabie's room, there was blood found on clothing, the mattress, and carpet. Those blood samples are human and they don't match your daughter or a soul in the Mathews' home."

"What? I don't…I don't understand."

"Drake," Salizar's tone stiffens. "There is a third person involved. That person bled…a lot."

I feel my stomach crawling up my esophagus.

"And it wasn't Maurine or Robert? No one?" Drake

stands.

"No. What we obtained from the Mathews' home is third party. There was someone else involved that night."

I see thoughts swirling in Drake's eyes. Thoughts are swirling in my head as well. I have no fucking clue what the hell happened.

"Drake…think…please think. Was there anything, anything out of the ordinary—"

"I told you everything…the scarecrow!" Drake shouts.

Only our breath is heard in the otherwise silent room. Our gazes connect as Drake looks wildly at either of us.

"What? Scarecrow?" Salizar prompts Drake to sit. He obliges.

"The day before she went missing…the morning…Coty and I were playing I Spy. She mentioned she saw the scarecrow in the field. I took that thing down months ago. When we went back to look, it was gone. I assumed it was Jakabie, but now that I think about it…Jak would never be in the fields on a Sunday morning. They're always at church. They *never* missed a service."

Salizar shakes her head. "You're just now mentioning this?"

"So much happened. I didn't think anything of it."

My ignorant brother. Impatiently tucked himself away in the crop. He was to wait there until Drake and his daughter departed from the home for our little date. The neighbors would have been gone, and he'd be able to find the perfect hiding place. Apparently, he left the corn prior to them leaving the house. *So, he was breaking the rules well before.*

"So now you're thinking what?" Drake looks to the ceiling.

"Thinking? Graves, right now I know there are a five-year-old girl and an eighteen-year-old man missing. There were three people involved, and one of them was seriously injured…now you're telling me this mystery person could have been traipsing around the property the entire day."

"What if this person took both of them? What…" Drake rests his elbows on the table and places his thumbs between his teeth.

"I need you to think, Drake. Think hard. Don't tell me you've told me everything when I'm just now hearing about a goddamned disappearing scarecrow. That scarecrow may very well have all the answers."

Drake plants his face in his hands.

I can't deal with another emotional breakdown, so I take my leave to the porch. *What happened?*

Did Jakabie witness the abduction and try to intervene? Was the blood Carter's blood? Why was there blood in Jakabie's room? If Carter killed Jakabie…why was there someone else's blood in his room?

"No. There's no way." My mind races. My thoughts bounce around yet all land on the same reality, the blood must be Carter's. "That crazy sack of shit…" Jakabie must have intervened that night. Carter must have been wounded and now I'm stuck here to speculate. Did Carter kill Jakabie? Did he kidnap him with Coty? I don't know what the hell my brother would want with something like Jakabie. His parents should have tossed that shit in the burn barrel when he was still a tot. No. Carter wouldn't have kept the kid breathing, he was of no use to him. But what if…

"Hey." Drake walks out on the porch.

"Oh. Hey, you startled me."

He runs his hands through his hair, nostrils flared and mouth agape.

"Everything okay?" I ask.

"Holy shit, Ash. This is big."

We're joined by Salizar.

"Tell me," I prompt him to continue.

"What was Jakabie really doing that night? What if…what if he was just trying to stop someone from taking Coty—"

"But, where is he?" I interrupt. "If Jakabie rescued Coty from this mystery abductor, then where is he now? Why would a hero run away? And where is Coty? We know Jakabie is still near, he's making meals in your clinic with your supplies, but where is Coty if Jakabie saved her?"

"And where is the true perpetrator?" Salizar follows up.

Drake shakes his head. "I just don't know how much more I can take. I can't handle this any longer."

*You and me both.*

Salizar and Drake carry on their mindless rambling—theories and how this all impacts poor Drake before she leaves once more.

My own theories are choking my morning. I can't anymore. It's time to run. It's time to leave for Juarez. It's time to cut my losses, and if I leave now with what reserves I have, another opportunity may be in my future.

After telling Drake I have to meet with my boss, I'm

driving home. There's a feeling of relief. It's over. I may have failed miserably, yet time is on my side, and I'm sure Momma will have a margarita waiting for me.

My packed bag is waiting for me by the door inside my home. A shower to freshen up for the drive and I'll be on my way.

In the bathroom, steam rolling and hair lathered, I open my eyes to darkness once I've rinsed. "Dammit." Assuming the light has burned out, I turn the water off and step from behind the curtain.

There's no sense in replacing it, so I'll open the door and let the natural light shine in.

Another completely legitimate and real emotion is fear. My path to the door is obstructed by another human. Someone tall and broad stands between me and the doorway—my escape. *Carter*.

"Oh my god! Car…Carter, is that you?" I step back. "Is that you? I thought…I thought you fucked me over. Turn on the light."

Silence.

"Carter?"

"Nope." The deep response sends me stepping backward, gripping the wall behind me.

"What the…who are you? What do you want?"

A low chuckle has my fists ready to pummel the dude in the face.

"Where is your bother? Where is the girl?"

"Who the fuck are you?"

The grip around my throat is so intense I feel as though he may lift me from the ground. "Please!"

"There's no use begging, my friend. Only answers will spare your life. *Ou est-il?*"

"What? I don't know!"

His entire body weight crushes me into the wall behind me. I'm defenseless. Something cold eases its way along my right side, stopping just below my ribs.

"*Es-tu pret?*"

"I don't speak French, fucker—"

"You are seconds away from being opened up like a gift at a six-year-old's birthday party…your insides will cover this floor. Do you know now? Do you?" His thick, rich tone is mildly intoxicating. *This is it.*

Every muscle in my body relaxes into him. My face rests aside his and our breaths share the same pace and air. I'm ready for it. *End me now. End it all.* "I told you…I don't know. Do it."

His lips trace over mine, soft and full. And then he releases me.

"You haven't heard from him? Nothing?"

"No." I remain affixed to the wall.

"And yet your bag is packed, waiting by the door?"

"Turn on the light—"

"The bag!" he yells.

"I have no idea where Carter is. I thought maybe…maybe he kept the girl for more money. I don't know. I can't stay here hoping he'll magically appear. It won't be long until these pigs piece this shit together and have me in handcuffs. I'm leaving."

"No. Not today."

"What are you going to do? Kill me? Do it now, fucker."

I hear nothing until his breath is inches from my face. "The offer still stands, beautiful. Bring me the girl before I find her, and leave this place with your fortune. But if you attempt to escape without fulfilling the deal, you will die screaming."

"I don't know where Carter is. He could be anywhere."

"No, he's here. He's somewhere here."

"How do you know this?"

He laughs. "Your brother hasn't made a phone call or touched his account in days. He is somewhere here."

"Shit."

"Yes. And you would know best where to find him, yes?"

"Get out of my house so I can get dressed. I need to think."

He kisses my wet cheek. "You are a dangerous, beautiful breed, Ashlyn Ramirez. Please, bring me the girl so I don't have to do bad things to you."

I chuckle. "The fuck makes you think I don't want you to do bad things to me? Also, tell that bitch, Sherri, if she'd have told me she had an idea Carter was still lurking around here, I would have been spending my time more wisely trying to find him."

There's no response, only a partial silhouette of a man walking out of my bathroom door before he closes it behind him.

I smile while wrapping a towel around me and sitting on the edge of the tub. There aren't many places I can think of that Carter frequents or where he might hang out, especially if he's wounded or toting a wretched little spawn like Coty, but there's a chance he's nearby and that means there's a chance I can still pull this off before I escape south and away from this shithole for good.

Dressed and motivated, I head to my car. It feels good to decline Drake's call the instant the shit shows up on my screen. Of course, he calls right back. Rolling my eyes as I start the ignition, I bring the phone to my ear. "Hey, sugar."

*"Oh, god, Ashlyn!"* My heart races listening to him wail in the phone. Please don't say you've found Coty dead somewhere.

*"It's Biggles!"*

The review mirror captures my gleaming grin as I nearly burst into laughter. "Oh…oh no, bubba. What's, what's the matter with him?" My hand presses my lips together, sealing my glee within my mouth.

He's crying hysterically and possibly vomiting on the other end of the line. *"Ashlyn! He's been sac…Biggles has been sacrificed!"*

I have to take the phone from my face, as I'm laughing uncontrollably at this point. And then I smell an opportunity as I bring it back to my curled lips.

"Drake, baby-doll. What are you talking about? Biggles was just fine when I saw him last."

*"It's awful, Ash! It's…oh my god!"*

"Okay, sugar-bear. I'm on my way to you now. We're going to figure this out together."

So incredible is the scene coming into view as I approach Drake's house, that I decide my dagger has not only twisted, but has now completely eviscerated my victim. With his face planted in his palms, Drake walks aimlessly across his yard, oblivious to my presence. I've done this. I have reduced this man to this state and it is a scrumptious sight to behold. My anger is melting like butter in a skillet of sautéed Biggles. I'm now only motivated to finish the mission and escape. I can withdraw the dagger, at least a tad.

The closing car door captures his attention and sends him in my direction.

"Oh, you poor thing. Did the coyotes get him?" I raise my arms, wrapping them around his neck as he crumbles into me.

"No." His quivering shakes through me and I'm certain he's completely crushed. "It's disgusting, Ashlyn."

I was so consumed with meal preparation plans I hadn't put much into clean-up on the day I disposed of Biggles. I honestly believed my departure would come before Drake went snooping around his property and found the crime scene.

"Show me, Drake." I kiss his damp cheek. Salt and sadness trace my tongue…*oh, those tasty tears*. And yet, I'm done with torturing this creature for sport.

"It's nothing you want to see, Ash." Monotone words are as expressionless as the face looking at me— blank and begging for an afternoon of privacy and a week's worth of prescription of narcotics. *He's done.*

"Show me, Drake."

Hand in hand, we walk to the back of the barn. A large, circular blood stain in the center of the cement barn floor boasts the dehydrating pelt of Biggles in the center. Just adjacent is a sloppy pile of entrails, clad in flies and debris. The scene does appear sadistic in nature.

Attempting to appear appalled, I shake my head. "Drake. This is madness. Who would do such a thing?"

"The same sonofabitch who has my daughter…Jakabie Mathews. He's just out there. Fucking with me. I think…I think he took Coty that night. Someone tried to stop him and he killed them for it. And now…" His pulsating throat glistens in tears and the sun. "And now I'm wondering how I'm going to find Coty. I found my cat like this…how will I find her? I can't imagine…I don't want to think about what he did to her."

Initially, my cruelty was a byproduct of the mission…the job. This little number was just me being extra. But now, a piece of me wants him to know his daughter is not the centerpiece of some slasher scene. Even the cruelest of the cruel can offer some sense of mercy.

"Drake, where are you going?"

He walks away, hands in his pockets—kicking at the dirt as he looks toward the ground. "I guess I should call the authorities. They're going to want to know about this. This means Jak was here…literally at this house recently and I didn't even know."

"You're not safe, Drake."

He turns, shrugging. "I don't…I don't even care anymore, Ash."

Drake sits on the porch, speaking with an investigator on the phone while I prepare some tea. My mind has wandered elsewhere. Although, the death of dear Biggles may be just the diversion I need to lurk about the shadiest bits of Eva and Elkhart, looking for my brother, Carter.

Carter is a patron of taverns and trailer-park poker tables in the area, but he's a bit of a wanderer and has few true friends.

Some nights he sleeps on my couch, and I'm clueless where he sleeps the other nights. Finding him may prove difficult, but I'm overwhelmingly motivated. I need answers and he's going to give them to me.

Tea prepared, I meander outdoors to find a solemn

Drake, sitting motionless in his rocker.

I enquire as to when the plethora of piglets is to arrive…again. He sighs and takes his glass, telling me he spoke with Alvarado, as Salizar wasn't available and someone would follow up as soon as possible.

I leave Drake to his despair and return to clean and kill the time. The disposal screams as it chews up the remainder of the enchiladas I prepared. Something tells me they aren't going to be eaten anyway. Dishes, dusting, and brainstorming are abruptly interrupted by a concerned Drake, traipsing through the kitchen door.

A bottle of rum is produced from the cabinet. I oblige him by handing over a canned Coke from the fridge and a glass of ice.

Drink prepared, Drake sits at the table. His buzzing phone seems to startle him.

"Hello?" Drake's flaccid expression hardens hastily within seconds. "Priority? What…what do you mean? You fuckers race out here every time someone farts, but this isn't a priority?"

His hand presses into his forehead as he listens to whoever is on the other end. "What? Tied to my daughter's investigation? I don't understand, dude. I can't…I seriously can't. I'm telling you that Coty, the same little girl who is missing, had a pet. That pet is now in pieces in my barn. Someone splatter-movie killed him and left the remains out there for me to find…and he has my daughter."

Eyes widening, he shakes his head defeatedly, peering past me to anything else. "Cool. You do that."

I'm hungry—starving, for information. He presses end, sets the phone aside and sips his drink silently.

"You okay, sugar-bear—"

"No! Ashlyn. That's seriously the most stupid question you could ask."

Oh, my. Someone may have dropped a testicle. *Fierce.* "Sorry." I wait pathetically for his apology, my back to him as I place dishes in the cabinets. It doesn't come.

"Drake, I know you're hurting. I understand I didn't know her as much as I'd have loved to, but that doesn't mean I don't care. And Biggles…" my voice cracks—perfect timing, "…he was my little friend, too."

His shoulders drop. "Ash, I know. I get it. I know." The irritation in his voice is strong. I'm loving it. "Right now, I don't think I have the emotional fortitude to handle how this may or may not be affecting you. I can't. I love you, and I do care about your feelings, but it's all I can do to brush my fucking teeth. I can't worry if I'm going to say the wrong thing or act too sad or too anything. My daughter's gone. Tell me how to act. Or better yet, give me a fucking break."

This bitch. My days have been spent drying his pantywaist tears and cuddling him while he works through his precious feelings, and now he wants to come at me like I've been a burden. "I understand."

"I'm sorry, Ash."

"Don't be. I think a night or so with your feelings and a mixed drink or two will be therapeutic. You know I'm a call away."

"You're leaving? Now?"

"Yes. You need this. You'll thank me." Walking to him, I kiss his shocked face. "But please let me know what comes of this when the officers do decide to show."

Arms folded like a scolded child, he stares at the

wall. "Well, I don't know when that's going to be. They're on-scene with another high-priority, and the assholes can't even tell me if it's directly related to Coty's case…only that they still haven't found Coty."

*Geppetto!* The hogs must have already stumbled across my side project, Alberta Gonzalez. Dread or instinct—something is demanding I run from Drake's. *Waddle away, flightless moth.* "Well, there you have it. You'll have some time to think without being concerned with me or feeling as though you need to entertain my presence. This is me, giving you a break." I blow him a kiss, keys in hand, as I walk backward to the door.

He appears devastated—as if I just ran over his puppy. *Nope, but there is certainly more than one way to skin a cat.*

My window of opportunity is rapidly closing. There's nothing more to do except find Carter, get the girl to the big butch wolf, and get the hell out of here.

"Ash!" Just as I'm opening the door, he's tripping over himself to get down the steps.

"Yes."

"Come back. Please come back tonight."

"Call me later. Love you, Drake."

There's an anxious itch within my core telling me to leave. Drake is left standing stunned in the dusty driveway as I tear away slowly like an old bandage.

Carter is my brother…my own brother—and I haven't a clue where the fuck to begin looking for him.

Dirt roads and big skies are good for dusty vehicles and clear thoughts. As children, much of mine and Carter's relationship was unspoken. When space was needed, it was apparent, and I did my best to provide it so he could break a window or kill something and heal from one of Daddy's beatings or something some asshole said at school. Other times though, not often, but sometimes, Carter was in clear need of company. I knew where to find him. Migrative, yet habitual, he'd always be in one of several places.

Some of my fondest memories come from a foundation of a clubhouse tucked within tall trees and foliage next to a tiny stream about five minutes from our house. After school, we'd race from our tin-box home and through the pasture just north of the trailer park. The clubhouse was our own little world. We'd share secrets and make pacts, and at times I felt something within. I felt like perhaps I was connecting and understanding the words people used to describe their emotions. Momma explained to us how emotions were a trickster's tool. Most all displays of emotion are fake, she'd say. Learn to understand and control genuine emotion, and master the art of conveying artificial emotion, and all the world around us would be a stage for our string puppets. We could manipulate and take as we saw fit.

The clubhouse was different. The emotion was genuine, and in our own little world, it was okay to show it. Carter's eyes would bulge and come alive with excitement when he'd speak of finding and dismembering a new nest of baby birds or a possum playing dead.

I'd tell him how I wanted nothing more than to grow up pretty enough to get what I needed from the world around us so I didn't have to eat mac and cheese all my life. He always complimented me on my beauty. We were normal…*our normal.*

One afternoon I visited the clubhouse alone. The emotion within me seemed genuine, yet I didn't understand it or why I was so impacted by simple words. When Carter finally joined me, he found me writhing in anger. I told him I was taunted at school. I was called trash, a half-breed, and told by Tanya Garcia that my own father hated me so much that he had to be completely drunk to come to my home and see me. I'd done nothing to instigate the verbal assault, but I'm assuming my anger burned so hot because her words were true.

The following day at school, the elementary students were tasked with cleaning the high school football field bleachers and stands. Tanya was *accidentally* tripped while descending from the top of the bleacher steps. She tumbled several sections down before coming to a battered halt. A broken wrist, collarbone, and multiple rib fractures and bruises had her out of school for nearly two weeks. The concussion she sustained only condemned her theory that she'd been pushed from behind by the deviant, Carter Ramirez.

Carter and I delighted in his depiction of the events. He mimicked her screech and her cries perfectly. We laughed so hard our bellies ached. It was real. That too…was real. I never told him when other students were mean to me. I didn't want him sent away to the delinquency center like Matt Barret and April Harmon. But I was convinced he'd always have my back when needed. Now, this.

Near the blacktop road to town, I find I'm lost. My brother is more twisted than the vinery that held our childhood playhouse among the trees together, but his loyalty was something I've never before questioned.

And now, as I need him more than ever, I'm clueless as to where to look. Our clubhouse and the days of childhood innocence are long gone.

My vehicle always sits on a full tank of gas…always. I'm probably just shy of that now, but the instant I'm in town I pull into the little store on Main Street. Every time I'm here I think this place has a different name and the pumps are archaic as fuck, so I have to go inside to pay.

Surprisingly, no one is staring me down as I top off the tank. The sun beats down on me as if it's telling me to get back inside my car and find Carter…find Coty, and escape.

The cool air whisks my hair back and brings with it hints of different scents and the heavy gaze of Girtie from behind the counter as I enter the establishment. Her eyes are begging for interaction. She could converse with a stump if the stump appeared interested. Her mental capacity is more than likely that of a tree stump.

I ignore her and walk to the cooler for a bottle of water. I continue ignoring her as I make my way toward the Starbursts.

Girtie smiles as I approach and I swear the bitch has more acne scars than teeth. A combination of a lifetime of economic challenges and family friendly DNA, Girtie is easy to despise. I could see her from afar and know I hate her without ever hearing a syllable whistle through the gap where her front tooth should be.

I set my items down and offer a passive smirk.

"Howdy, Ashland."

"It's Ashlyn, actually."

"Oh. Well, hello to both of ya!" She chuckles,

glancing at the price tags. "Will this be all? It's two eighty-seven."

"I had fuel. Four dollars."

Mouth agape, she stares out the large glass window toward my vehicle.

"So, I'm assuming that means I owe you six dollars and eighty-seven cents?" I snap.

"Oh." Wide-eyed, she chicken-pecks the keys. "I assume it does."

If I were ten years old again, I'd rip this bitch off.

"So, Ashland, is your brother working for Gilly Thompson?"

I roll my eyes. "I wouldn't know."

"Oh…seems you two is real close, so I figured—"

"Figured what? Incest? Not everyone born from small-town America is into copulating with their family members."

"Huh? Insects? No, I meant like tearing down them old houses, ya know? There's a few boys out there on Six-Mile Road in the morning on my way in. But then I been seeing Carter's car there a couple times at night."

"What? What the fuck did you just say?" I lean on the counter to her. "What did you just say to me?"

"Oh. Well, that's a tacky mouth."

"Have you seen him? It's important. When was the last time you saw that fucker's car?"

She stares at me as if I've just asked her to count from ten backward.

"Please. Girtie, think…it's important. My brother has been missing."

"No, he ain't. I just seen him yesterdee evening. His car was parked out at that demolition right next to the porta potties."

"Yesterday, you say?" My heart is racing.

"Yes, ma'am. He was there yesterdee and the day before that. I'd put my money on it, he'll be back again tonight."

I'm grinning widely. "Oh…oh, Girtie. Dear, sweet Girtie, thank you! Keep your change." I race to my vehicle.

The assholes weren't looking before, but they are now as my tires smoke and I tear from the parking lot, the underside of my car striking the street as I enter traffic.

Speeding from town and down the highway, it's a good five minutes until I'm seeing the green portable bathrooms to the right of me that Girtie was talking about. They sit next to a partially deconstructed home about a quarter of a mile off of the highway.

I slow only to make the turn and then race for the vehicles parked there. Dust flies as I slam on the brakes in the driveway of the dilapidated home. Two white men, appearing in their twenties, look from their lunch pails toward me as if they're under the impression that I am insane.

"Hey!" I yell out as I exit the vehicle. "Carter Ramirez."

The look of pure confusion appears to be tattooed.

"Do you know Carter Ramirez? Does he work here?"

"No…no, ma'am." One of the guys finally speaks while sitting on the cement steps of the home under the porch awning. "We work for our Uncle Gilly. Just a summer gig before we go back to school."

"Bullshit. Carter's car has been seen here for two nights—"

"Who is Carter?" The man stands. "Someone's been lurking around here, stealing from our coolers at night. Who the heck is Carter?"

I smile. My hand rests aside his baby-face. That always seems to calm a man. "Oh no. You poor little fellas. Did someone take your Cheetos and Sprite? What a shame."

His glare transforms into a smirk and then a smile.

"Can I make you boys a deal?" They're both standing now. "You're going to follow me to park my vehicle and bring me back here. When the thief returns tonight, I'll be here to deal with them."

"Ha. You? What're you going to do?" the smaller guy asks.

My smile fades. "Whatever I have to." My tone slaps the expression from his face. "And in return for keeping your little mouths shut...I'll give you some cash for a month's supply of Cheetos and Sprite." I slide two one-hundred dollar bills from my billfold.

His arms cross as he grins. "Fine, but we drink Gatorade...not Sprite, and I don't like Cheetos."

# Part III: Closure

# Chapter Eleven

### Drake

I shouldn't have touched her. Of the millions of memories housed in my brain, that's my last one of my mother. Her comforting hands, perfectly clasped and boasting a glimmering diamond, were inches from mine in my darkest hour. A mother's love is irreplaceable, but that day I realized it wasn't in the shell before me in the casket. My fingertips traipsed along rubbery, cold death and I fractured from the inside out.

To be loved is to provide a window-viewing of a tarnished soul and expect nothing in return but grinning lips, spilling affection freely, and deep-rooted connection in every touch because they adore the view.

My father's love was there. Like the leaves on the trees outside my childhood bedroom window, his affection showed thicker and more vibrantly during happy times wrapped in warmth and lacking cold tribulation.

My mother's love was big. Her love was larger than the night sky we'd often admire. Stargazing gigglers, lying atop a quilt on the green grass and muttering more wishes than the night could keep up with.

My mother taught me to look for beauty first, and if it wasn't there, then to change perspectives before turning away. She taught me that a woman will never be found by simply opening a car door or pulling out a chair. *'She'll never need your permission, but she'll gobble your encouragement.'* She allowed me to see the world through the eyes of a little boy who was loved and lifted up by her wisdom and steadfast strength.

I never knew what it was to be alone until the day they left me. They disappeared in a chaotic cluster of odd words and swirling circumstances that weren't absorbable at the time. The accident was just that, an accident. The night's heavy rain and unfamiliar roads had my father taking a left turn rather than right. He drove down a boat ramp…twenty-five miles an hour into frigid lake water. They submerged rapidly and were pulled from the lake's grasp just in time for would-be rescuers to say there was nothing to be done. They'd pulled my parents from the water only minutes after they'd entered it, yet a piece of my soul remained submerged.

To be lonely, my lonely, was to crave companionship while knowingly settling for something imposturous.

Selfish…yes, I was selfish. The instant Renee brought news of a potential life within her womb, I felt the murky waters parting…opening. There was this excitement around the idea of creating something, someone, to love and to love me the way I felt love before the accident.

She cried. Renee's tears represented something I couldn't understand, and therefore couldn't comfort. Red marker in hand, I drew the thick, red X through the Wednesday marking week 27. I knew from that point on…there was a chance. This little person had a legitimate chance.

The week before Coty was to arrive, I entered the bedroom to find Renee curled on the bed. The window was open, and a soft breeze tickled the curtains behind her. Her gaze was hollow, yet each tear was saturated in obvious pain.

We'd talked of the options. Regardless of what I say or whom I say it to, I know Renee never truly considered anything other than life…other than Coty. She did that for me, not her. She knew it would have crushed me and there was little left to crush. That's what I mean when I say she loved me with what she had. I used her as a vessel. She gifted me the most precious gift imaginable. And she left. I'll never understand her mind, but I could never hate her after what she gave me…I'll never truly hate her.

*Now*. Now I'm beyond alone. I've felt the pain of loss and being alone but this is not that. This constant alteration of the mentality. To hope, to despair, to feel guilty for feeling despair…continuously wondering how long she cried…how long she suffered while trying to ensure her laughter is permanently embedded in my head. I can't lose that.

It's true. I'm selfish. And embracing that, taking it

in, will make the act of departing from this world less taxing once they find my baby. I can't live without my sunshine…I don't want to, and I won't. I'll go too.

Ashlyn's been a foundation of support. She isn't a vessel. She isn't a starter-kit. She'll hurt. I'm sure this final, selfish act will hurt her tremendously, and for that, I am desperately sorry, but I don't have the strength to be anymore.

The blood coursing through me now is laced with a vengeful toxin. My baby will be brought home and laid to rest. And when I find him…when my hands are on him…the thoughts, the way his face twists my mind unhealthily is nauseating.

They're finally coming. There's something sour in the way the white sedan inches toward my home. I know it carries officers and news as I watch it creep closer and come into view. There's a hesitation in the way it approaches, like a child being summoned for a spanking.

It pulls in the drive and Salizar and Alvarado exit. Grim expressions have become a common theme, but these are the grimmest. *Is this it?*

The spasm in my throat makes it impossible to swallow as I stand.

"Dr. Graves," Alvarado says as he approaches.

"Yeah."

"May we come in?"

"Yes." The piece of me aching to demand information is silenced by the majority of me—the horrified part.

Inside, I'm prompted to sit. Just as the courage has formulated the words, *Did you find her*, Alvarado speaks.

"We're not here about Coty, Drake."

My breath escapes me. My insides feel as though they could erupt from my face. "What? Why? Why are you here then?"

Salizar seats herself across from me. I haven't a clue what the hell else they could want, unless someone else is hurt too. *Ashlyn!* "Ashlyn! Is Ashlyn—"

"We're not here about Ashlyn," She continues, resting her hand on my arm. "Not long after I left you this morning…a 911 call directed us back to this area."

"Another call? Who?"

"Donita Gonzalez called."

"Ms. Gonzalez's niece?" Salizar smiles softly and nods. "No! Is she okay? Tell me Alberta Gonzalez is okay!" My voice cracks as I stand.

"Please sit, Drake." Alvarado's massive hand on my shoulder prompts me to sit.

"Drake, Ms. Gonzalez was found by her niece this morning." Salizar attempts to remain calm and soothing.

"Found?" I bark from across the table.

"She was found with several empty vials of insulin, dead on her couch in an apparent suicide."

Salizar's words circle atop my head like sink water swirling down the drain. As they slide in, nothing about them makes sense other than the fact that my friend might be dead. "No."

"Drake. Her last communication was with you. She canceled plans."

Two tears etch their way from my eyes. Alberta Gonzalez deserves so much more than that. My tear reserve is all but gone. "Ms. Gonzalez was here just yesterday morning. She came here for me and she was coming back last night to cook for us."

"Us?" Alvarado interjects.

"Ashlyn and I."

"And then she sent you this text message? A text you didn't respond to?" Salizar continues.

The text, as well as the cancellation, was atypical of Ms. Gonzalez. But nothing has been typical as of late. "I was on a house call. I saw a patient yesterday because I thought it'd help to clear my mind. When I got the text, rather than a call, I thought it was strange, but thought maybe she was overwhelmed. I didn't call or reply for that reason. When Alberta wanted to talk…we'd talk for hours. When she didn't, she'd let me know about it."

Salizar sighs. "Drake…this suicide comes—"

"She didn't commit suicide," I interrupt her. "I don't…I don't care what it looks like or even if she left a note." Salizar's forehead creases, her lips curl slightly and she nods as if she's confirming she agrees with me. "I know her. I *know* Alberta Gonzalez, and she wouldn't have done this. It had to have been an accident or…"

"An accident?" Alvarado steps closer. "Dr. Graves, she's been a diabetic for nearly twenty years. This was no accident."

"Fine. It may not have been an accident, but I'm telling you that you need to look at this one closely before you write it off as self-inflicted."

"What makes you so certain?" Salizar asks.

"Ms. Gonzalez is highly spiritual. She's also very conservative and extremely outspoken on her beliefs. She's denounced the act of suicide, and how it might impact one's mortal soul, on countless occasions."

"Dr. Graves, could that have been a cover?" Alvarado squats to eye-level. "Sometimes in our profession, we see suicidal people who claim to despise it as a cover-up. Perhaps she was hurting inside, and with Coty—"

"Of course she's hurting inside. We all are. I'm sure you've seen several of these scenarios you're painting, but how many of them are sixty-seven-old first-generation immigrants who fought like hell for a shot at the American dream, and then fought like hell and kicked cancer's ass? That woman loves life…" It appears as though my tear reserve isn't dry after all. They're now streaming. "She loved it, and she told me how much she loved it every chance she got. She didn't hurt herself."

Alvarado stands. "You were on a house call yesterday, you say? Where?"

"The Garrison Ranch. Just east of Boise City, Oklahoma."

"Where was Ashlyn?" His question puzzles me.

"Here. She's been staying here with me."

"Where is she now?" There's more to his prodding than I'm comfortable with. They're attempting to piece and link together multiple mysteries and are looking to cast blame now that things aren't fitting. It's unnerving. "She left for the night."

"Left?" he digs.

"Yes. She left. She has a home and a life outside of me. She can't just sit around while I sulk. She's missed work and—"

"Work?" Alvarado smiles slyly.

"Yeah. She's a nurse."

"I'm aware." There's an antagonistic quality to his

tone and words and the way he stands above me. "One year? You two have dated for one year. Correct?"

"Yeah. About that long."

"Drake." Salizar's softer tone is much more inviting. "We're only sifting through each detail. Ashlyn Ramirez has been here through the duration of the investigation. This is natural."

"You're too kind, Salizar." Alvarado chuckles.

"My girlfriend is a good person. You all waste so much time chasing pointless shit just because you're lost."

"Really?" Alvarado's arms cross.

"Yeah. You still haven't found Jakabie. You have no clue where that boy is so you pacify the hours with random flavors of the day. Today just happens to be Ashlyn."

"Show us the barn, Graves," Salizar interrupts.

I lead them to where I found my family pet. Coty loved Biggles. Coty loved Ms. Gonzalez. My life has dissolved and there aren't words to describe what is left.

At the barn, I only visualize their reaction, not the scene itself. They both appear disgusted, and even their expressions and disturbed mannerisms are enough to send me back to the porch.

I wait in the fading light of another day. An orange glow cascades over the corn and my yard. Like the crops around me, I will be gone when this very area is dusted in the frigid white of winter. There's something comforting in that thought.

The sun has settled in by the time the officers return. Salizar holds an evidence bag.

"We buried what we could, Drake. There's a mound

near the back of the barn. We washed the floor clean, too."

"Thank you. You didn't have to do that." I stand.

"We'll be in touch—"

"Salizar. Every time I see your vehicles coming toward my house, I'm gutted. I don't want to see you again until you find her. Please."

She nods. "Keep your phone on, boy."

"Drake." A sweating Alvarado steps forward. "Take care of yourself."

They leave me to the night.

My house is empty but my brain is crawling with thoughts and memories. *I need her.*

The phone rings a few times in my ear before I hear Ashlyn's voicemail. I opt to text her and pace—awaiting her return call. When the call doesn't come, I call again.

I shower, hoping she'll call while I clean. She doesn't. This is atypical. When Ashlyn is working graveyard shifts at the hospital she'll call me hours later, but outside of work, she's easy to contact. There was an undeniable irritation when she left, but I can't imagine her being angry at me…not now.

A third attempt goes unanswered and I'm anxious, dressed in shorts and shirt and walking to my vehicle.

Ashlyn is the only constant I have. My brain tosses tidbits of random happiness out among a collage of depression, anger, and confusion. Those pieces of pleasure have Ashlyn's face on them. Ideas of drifting and giving in are quelled only by a desire to find Coty…and Ashlyn's ambitious outlook for our future.

I drive responsibly down the dirt road, taking the opportunity to give the area a glance-over…*maybe I'll spot a devil.*

Once in town, I creep by the hospital first. There's no sign of her vehicle.

Her house is only a few blocks over. Dark cars line the dark street and dark homes. Ashlyn's house is the darkest.

Still, I pull into the driveway and kill the engine. "Where are you?"

Carter's vehicle isn't here either, but something lures me from my vehicle and has me knocking on the front door. My gentle knocks nudge the door ajar.

I step from the night and into complete black. "Hel…hello?"

I'm a firm believer in instinct. When something snatches my breath briefly…or I feel something sinister eyeing me from an undisclosed area…I simply take my leave. Why am I not doing that now?

There's an evil housed in these walls. Maybe I'm only seeing it now that I'm blinded, or maybe it's only now here.

The texture of the wall tickles the tips of my fingers as I quietly fumble for the light switch. I flip it on, expecting to find some monster…I see nothing but a cozy living room. The light does not extend into the rooms leading from the living room. I stare at the hallway as if it's a dark cave, crawling with insidious creatures.

"Dude. Chill." *She must be with Carter.* This is difficult for her too.

There's a small half bathroom just off the living room. I step in and close the door to take a piss before I leave.

Hands washed, I open the bathroom door.

Breath…snatched. The living room light is off. The only light in the home is the light of the small bathroom I'm standing in. It bleeds dingy and yellow into the darkness.

*What the fuck?* I could run for the front door. I could close the bathroom door and lock it…hope for the best. Or I could be logical. The light burnt out. This is nothing. I'm a man. Nothing lurks here that I can't assess accurately and handle. There are no insidious things here, creatures or otherwise. This is the home of the woman I love. I step into the darkness, walking casually toward the door.

If something wicked is watching me, it won't see me panic.

Guided by pale street light through the tiny window in the front door, I walk confidently until my path is obstructed and I'm falling. I catch myself, there's no impact. Scrambling to the door and the light switch, I'm dizzied to find the light is working properly. Either it spontaneously turned itself off…or I'm not alone.

There's a bag on the floor—a bag I'm only now noticing. My hand is on the doorknob. I'm inches from exiting. *What's in the bag?*

Hastily, I rush to it and unzip the duffle bag to find familiar clothing items. Ashlyn's passport sits atop a dress shirt I've seen her wear multiple times. She hasn't mentioned a trip, and leaving now wouldn't make sense.

Her beautiful face peers up at me from the passport…and then it's gone, swallowed in black. It's pitch-black once more. Someone has flipped the switch…again. *Fight or flight.*

"Who the fuck is here?" I roll on my butt, looking

blindly through the darkness. I couldn't care less how I look at this point. If it were Ashlyn here with me, she would have responded, and it's common knowledge that her brother is batshit crazy.

Jumping to my feet, I race for the door and slam it behind me. In my car, I attempt to call Ashlyn once more as I pull away from her home—again…nothing.

I'm lost as to what to do. If Carter's crazy ass is in her home, then where the hell is she? The idea that she would leave has me peeling what raw nerve I have left. Losing her…even the thought of it is pulverizing, when only an hour ago I believed there was nothing more to pulverize. Perhaps a premature departure from this world isn't in my future. Maybe there is something left in my humanity tank. I have to find her. She's the only light left in me. I need to find Ashlyn.

# Chapter Twelve

### Ashlyn

I imagine Drake—mangled just off of the side of the road—bleeding and disfigured. I envision him the way my father was depicted to me in his final moments…in pieces but breathing. Every time that sonofabitch calls…again, my thumbs mentally sink into his eye sockets…his screams fill my ears. How can I not hate him right now? His persistence is excruciating. He's a virus. He's herpes in the worst way and I want to be rid of him forever. Each time I find it within me to muster compassion or even empathy…I'm slapped by his inability to fuck off. I told him to leave me be for the night and here he is, calling again…*flaring up*. He makes it easier to understand why my brother kills for fun.

There isn't much left of the house I'm waiting in. The walls are stripped to the support beams and pipes and lines are exposed. The flooring below me is subfloor. The moon illuminates dusty piles of swept pigeon shit. I sit in the corner on an old stool, hopeful my prize will come. If Carter doesn't come to me sometime tonight, I'll be forced to walk down the road to my vehicle. This house must have been built in the early 1900's. It's being deconstructed with little regard to its history. I'm sure this little home has housed several low-income tragedies, but none of that will be remembered once those people are dust and each nail has been stripped.

I'll be different. My mark on the world will be thick and permanent.

I'm curious as to why Carter has chosen to scavenge from Igloo coolers rather than head north. His injuries from the altercation with Jakabie must be extreme.

My phone buzzes again. Drake's name appears. If I were at home I'd answer and press play on my DVR…the sounds of ventilator and monitor alarms from *Grey's Anatomy* would fill my home and I'd tell the idiot I was at the hospital. But alas. I'm not there and I'm in no mood to conspire or hear his annoying voice anymore tonight.

My impatience is boiling by the time I hear a familiar engine. Carter's crappy car. I'm delighting in the possibility of answers. My future is approaching…I'm desperate to know what it consists of. Will I live richly in Mexico…carefree to construct my next mastermind of a manipulation…or will I flee there to beg my mother to add me to the roaches scurrying about her shabby Juarez home?

I peer out the open window as Carter's car comes to a complete stop. At last. This is *something*.

Quietly slipping from the front door, I watch him exit the vehicle and rush to the coolers near the porch. He moves swiftly…he doesn't appear to be wounded at all.

"Hola Mijo!" Trotting down the steps to the vehicle, I watch Carter trip over his own feet and fall to the ground as I reach into the vehicle and retrieve the keys, tucking them safely in my pocket. "You motherfucker. You have so much explaining…" As I step closer, peering down, I find the person looking up at me isn't Carter at all, but that jackass Jakabie. "What the hell?"

"Oh," he mutters, scooting backward as my inner rage boils.

"Why the *fuck* are you here in my brother's car?" He freezes, his eyes wide as I stand above him. His inability to do anything but stare up at me like an invalid fucktard has my hand raising.

He tucks his head and raises his arms in defense, but that's useless against my rage. A firm grasp on his thick brown hair with one hand, and I'm slapping and pounding that yelping face with the other. He scrambles to break free, but that only angers me further.

Moments later, breathing heavily, I stand above a crying, pathetic useless excuse for a human. My palms ache from striking him.

"Please. Please stop."

"Shut up!" I force my words through clenched teeth as I crouch to him, making a fist and threatening to punch him as he lies flat on his back.

His gaze diverts and he stares toward the stars—lip quivering like the coward he is. If I didn't need something from him, the bones in my hands would break from the beating I'd unleash on this sniveling garbage.

I take his twitching, wet face in my grasp, squeezing it between my thumb and index finger as he attempts to mutter something.

"What's that? What did you just say to me, you little pussy?"

"Please," he whines, "don't touch me."

His words make me explode—shoving his face and smashing his head into the gravel behind him. Inches from his gaze, our eyes lock. "I'm going to do more than touch you, you ugly, stupid, pathetic piece of shit. I'll kill you!" My screech fills the night. "Do you hear me, Jakabie Mathews! I'll fucking kill you right now if you don't do exactly as I tell you!"

He cries. His eyes clench closed and his cry carries past me and over the surrounding area. I smile…just where I want him. Broken.

"Look at me."

He continues to cry. His tears gain him yet another open-handed slap to the face. *"Look at me!"*

"Please." He opens his flooded eyes.

"That's a good boy, Jakabie. Now…where is Carter?"

He only stares at me. No words.

"Jakabie. This is very important. I need you to tell me where Carter is so I don't have to hurt you."

Like a child who has just dropped his ice cream cone, his face grimaces and he wails out, "I don't know!"

Grabbing the front of his shirt, my fingers pinching skin in my grasp, I bring him to me.

"You're touching—"

"Shut up! Shut. The. Fuck. Up." His nose is but a millimeter from mine. "Where is he? *Where is he!*"

He only shakes his face at me.

His feet scramble from beneath him for footing as I

stand and lift him violently by the hair to face me. "Inside!"

Just inside the door, he turns to me. This six-foot, eighteen-year-old kid is shaking…fingers extended, hands held up, he quivers before me and it's precious. If all men crumbled at my command…oh what a world I would live in. "Jakabie."

"Please," he begs.

I chuckle, closing the door behind me. Moonlight shines through the windows and dances in his streaming tears.

"Jakabie…I don't want to hear the word *please* come out of your mouth again, young man. Do you understand me? All I want to hear from you is where Carter is. You tell me where he is and we can be friends again…okay?"

He slowly retreats backward into the darkness, away from me as I walk methodically toward him. A burst of laughter escapes my mouth as he falls back on his ass over a pigeon shit pile.

"Why?" His squeak has me squatting to him, peering into his frightened, moon-kissed eyes.

"Why what?"

"Why are you being mean to me?"

It's clear the mental ailments afflicting him mean I'm going to have to rethink my method of obtaining information. This is no man. It's a damn shame too. Jakabie is a cute kid. It's like…pulling up to a nice house with reasonable curb appeal, only to open the front door to find an inside that's stupid and lacking any sense or reasoning. "Mean to you? You think I'm being mean to you, Jakabie?"

"Please stop."

"Jaaaakabie. What did we say about that word? No more. Okay?"

"Yes…yes, ma'am."

"That's a good boy, Jak. Now, I'm going to ask you nicely. Where is Carter? If you tell me you don't know…we're going to have some real issues. Do you understand me?"

He's silent.

"Jakabie. I can only be patient for so long. I need you to answer me. I don't want to be *mean* to you. So, tell me, and tell me right now, where is Carter?"

It requires every ounce of self-control to not pummel him in the face as he says nothing.

*Something else*. My hand reaches slowly for his face.

"No. No, please don't touch." There's nowhere to scoot back as he's against the wall now.

"Yes. Oh, Jakabie. Sweet, stupid little Jakabie." He shakes, his eyes widening like an abused chihuahua on one of those ridiculous animal rights commercials as my hand nears his cheek. "All you have to do is tell me, and this can all be over. Just tell me."

"Please—"

"No more *please*!" I inch closer. "Jakabie, is Coty with Carter? Tell me she's okay. Is she alive?"

My hand withdraws, allowing him to calm and answer.

"I don't know where Carter is."

"Okay. Do you know where Coty is?"

The question has him whimpering again.

"Jakabie. Did you…did you hurt Coty? Tell me now."

His gaze diverts.

"Now! Or I'm going to touch you!"

"Oh!" He's startled and looking around. "Um."

"Tell me right now, Jakabie. Did you hurt Coty?"

"Y…yes," he mutters.

*Fuck.* What happened? What actually happened? Did this idiot actually kill Coty? Where the fuck is Carter?

"Enough! You will tell me right now. Where did you drive from? Just tell me that. Where did you drive from?"

He's scrambling, attempting to stand. "Tell me now! Where is it that you drove from? Are they there?"

Face to face, he covers his crying eyes with his hands.

"Jakabie, do you know what's going to happen to you? Do you have any idea?"

Like the small animals Carter tortured, Jakabie's eyes house a look of rampant fear. "Jakabie, I can save you. If you tell me what you've done…I'll help you. But you have to tell me."

"Save me from what?" he whimpers out between gasps.

"Oh, Jakabie…when they find out that you know where Coty is and you didn't tell me, they're going to send you to jail."

"No!"

"Yes!" I squeal happily. "And when they do, they'll touch you every day."

"Oh!" He appears to be on the verge of hyperventilation. Pulling his hair and looking around wildly.

Kill shot. "They'll touch you, Jakabie, they'll hurt you. Just like he did…just like Gary." I grin widely, waiting for my words to penetrate as I inhale his terror. It's delicious.

As our gazes meet, he loses expression. The fear fades, leaving nothing but blankness.

"I can help you, Jak—" He shoves me aside as he makes his way for the door. "Jakabie, no!"

He's mere feet from the exit when I grab his bicep from behind. His elbow catches my cheek as he turns wildly to break free. I watch him lose balance and fall, arms flailing as he strikes the back of his head on the windowsill before crashing to the floor—lifeless.

"No. No! Jakabie." I squat to him, producing my phone for a flashlight. He moans softly as I examine him. "I hate you. Oh my god, I hate you." I slap his flaccid face once more for good measure before glancing about the shithole for something to restrain him with. When he awakens we'll have a splendid time of touching torture until I get the answers I need.

In what was once a kitchen, I locate a modern toolbox and half a roll of duct-tape.

Jakabie is dragged by the hair from the door. A pigeon shit pillow elevates his head as I secure his hands and feet properly with tape. Soft moans ensure me he's nearly conscious as I bind him.

The night's heat has me exiting the dusty dump for water or Gatorade or whatever those boys left in their cooler. A few red Gatorades and fresh air and I'm recharged and ready for my victim to rile.

"Jakabie!" Dust hugs the moonbeams tracing his face as I kick his foot. He only moans softly. "Damn, son." I sit next to him, watching him breathe as if he's sleeping.

I'm churning inside. The answers I need are trapped

in this dude and he's knocked the fuck out. There's also a calming quality in knowing I'll have those answers if his dumb ass wakes up. He will. Daddy threw Carter in the bathroom once and he didn't wake up for hours after hitting his head on the tub. And Momma beat my Uncle Richard unconscious with a rubber mallet, but he woke up too. This guy will wake up.

My head rests against the wall behind me. It isn't long before I'm yawning. My eyes close and I imagine my mother's face when I arrive wealthy and resilient. There's nothing to do but wait and fight to keep from wandering into slumber.

Sleep isn't an option now. With sleep comes the possibility of dreams. Each dream has the possibility to trick me into irrational thinking. Stupid brain. There's no such thing as an emotional scar if it's covering a festering, necrotic wound. I should be sympathetic to Jakabie and his childhood trauma but I'm not. I too could have added such an event to my resume of childhood trauma had Carter not intervened.

The rain sounds different in my dreams. I was young. Too young to understand that fighting back was okay. Too young to understand that what was happening wasn't natural. Tapping on the tin roof—tiny pelting raindrops, soothed my childhood troubles away that night. Silent as a moccasin, my Uncle Richard slithered under my sheets, his forked tongue whispering strange words in my little ear.

His breath burned with a nauseating pungency of stagnant alcohol and blackened nubs for teeth. Frozen. I was incapable of movement. Cracked fingers and callused palms slid under my baggy t-shirt and over my belly as I gripped my stuffed teddy.

He told me I'd feel good but I felt only disgusted when his onion-scented tongue licked my cheek. I never heard Carter come in, but the lightning illuminated his presence as he stood over me and Uncle Richard. Just as his fingers were gliding under my waistband, Carter yelled at him. The lights came on and my drunken uncle sprang from my bed. He stumbled to the door, his fingers slid through the narrow opening just over the bottom door hinge. Carter took the opportunity to simply close the door.

Initially, the bones crunching and my uncle's screams startled me. But as Carter grabbed his belly in laughter, I too laughed. We delighted in Uncle Richard's agony as he begged us to release him.

His screaming eventually woke my mother. I'd never seen her truly angry before, but when I told her what happened, she used a rubber mallet to hit my uncle over the head until he went unconscious.

That night, Carter showed me a VHS of what Uncle Richard was trying to do to me. I didn't understand then what the two, oily people on the screen were doing, only that they were groaning, there was awful music, and their privates looked weird as they ground them together. I was disgusted that my uncle was trying to do such a thing to me.

Daddy came home the next day at my mother's insistence. Daddy, Carter, and Uncle Richard were gone for days, and when the subject was mentioned, I was told to hush by Momma.

Daddy dropped Carter off three days later and drove away…but Uncle Richard was gone. Momma told Carter that what happened was a teaching tool, but was to be kept to himself.

Days passed before I was able to pry the information from my brother in the clubhouse, but when he spilled, his eyes gleamed with excitement. He told me of how he and our father drove for nearly a day with Uncle Richard tied and covered in the bed of the truck. He said they laughed and ate pizza and Dad even let Carter drive when he got too drunk! But the real bonding came when they reached their destination.

In an isolated field, miles from civilization, Daddy let Carter pour the kerosene on my pleading uncle. Then Daddy let Carter choose...*mercy or match*. Mercy was a bullet before they set Richard ablaze. Carter said he didn't think twice. He said he and Dad laughed all the way home at how Uncle Richard screamed like a pussy while he burned to death.

Carter told me Daddy said Uncle Richard had no good teeth and they'd never be able to figure out who he was if they ever found his charcoaled ass! Momma eventually found out Carter told me and the three of us would get a good chuckle out of it in the mornings while getting ready for school. Mother was never fond of her brother and often referred to him as Dick. When Carter would take too long in the bathroom in the morning, or if he came home late after school, we would crack some joke about him being out somewhere roasting wieners and the three of us would laugh our asses off every time.

Those were the days. I miss her face. I need to find my brother, get this money, and get the hell out of here so we can be a family again. To do that, I need my buddy to wake up.

Moments later, my heavy head snaps upright as I nearly drift. I could stand and walk. Perhaps I should pour cold Gatorade on Jakabie and see if that revives him. I rest my eyes once more, allowing my pupils to bathe in the blackness.

"I need to go pee." The words stir in my head. "Please."

I fling my eyes open. "Goddammit!" Springing to my feet, I look about the dawn-lit room. I fell asleep. How could I have been so stupid? How?

"Ms. Ashlyn…"

"Shut up, Jakabie." I run to the window, fingers gripping the sill as if it's a cliffside, and stare out to see if we're still alone. We are.

It's then my gaze falls upon Jakabie's face. I'm initially taken aback by the swollen eyes and busted lip, but then I remember how angry he'd made me. *Serves him well*.

My phone says it's 06:17. This has to happen now if it's going to happen.

"Jakabie, no more games." I walk to him. "Where did you drive from?"

Dust scatters as he squirms beneath me…and then the crotch of his jeans darkens.

"What the fuck, dude?"

"I'm sorry!"

"You're just going to piss yourself? A piss-pants pussy?" I chuckle.

"I told you. I tried—"

"Shut the fuck up. I've tried really hard to be sweet to you. It isn't working. If you don't help me find Coty, then I'm going to do horrible, awful things to you. I'll hurt you so bad that—"

"I can't say it. I…I don't know how to tell you." His eyes plead.

"What? That's stupid, Jak. You're a real dumb dude. Anyone ever tell you that?"

"I can show you. I can take you there."

I grin, my gaze narrowing in on my prize. "Good. Now we're getting somewhere." I kneel to the trash at my feet. "Jakabie. Will you take me to Coty? Is she alive? Is she with Carter?"

Like three perfect O's his eyes and mouth only stare back at me as I raise my hand.

"No! Please don't hit me!"

"Is Coty with Carter?"

"Who is Carter?" His expression, the way he leans into his question from the filth below him…he really doesn't know.

"Carter…my brother. Carter was…he was playing with Coty and you took her from him—"

"What? No." Rage brews in his eyes. "Your brother? She was crying…I didn't mean to."

"What happened, Jakabie? No more bullshit. Tell me what happened that night." I lean over him, staring down on him like a hawk on a mouse.

"The crickets…I like crickets—"

"I don't give a fuck about crickets! What happened?"

"My window was a little bit opened so I could hear the crickets. But…but I heard Coty. Coty was crying. I ran. I just ran and saw a mister taking her and it wasn't Dr. Graves…wasn't Drake."

"What did you do, Jakabie?"

"I jumped on them. Both of them, like a tackle." He looks away and goes silent.

"And?"

"It hurt Coty." A crack in his voice is coupled with

a quivering lip. I swear this world could use a little testosterone. So many pathetic, whining weaklings, it's nauseating. "It hurt her when she fell down."

"Did it hurt Carter when you fell?" I prod.

"That man? No." He shakes his face. "I grabbed a big ol' rock and hit him in the head a bunch of times though." His nonchalant proclamation has me itching to kill him, but to hurt him before I do.

"You did what?"

"His gun landed in the ditch when he fell. I knew it was real 'cause it looked like my poppa's. I knew what he was gonna do when he got a hold of it, so I just hit him."

My face is blazing. I want his agony embedded in my brain for all my days. He'll scream for mercy before I'm done with him. "Then what?"

"Um. Coty was scared. Real scared, and her face was bleeding. There was a car up the road, so we ran to it and I put her there…she was crying when she dropped her doll, so I went back to get it." His eyes fill with tears. That's when I saw that man. He was crawling through the dirt."

"Okay. Okay, good. What happened to the man?"

"I picked him up and ran. I ran hard to my house. I tiptoed in and put him on my bed and got Momma's bandage kit. Then I seen what I done."

"What you *done?* What, Jakabie, did you do?"

He cries. "He wasn't…he wasn't breathing. He was dead. I killed him."

Controlling the rage within me is nearly impossible.

"I didn't…I didn't know what to do. So, I ran. I took that man and ran back to the car with Coty."

His pathetic pouty lips are so slap-worthy right

about now.

"Coty was crying so loud. She was screaming she wanted her daddy. So, I put that man in the rear-trunk of that car, kissed Coty, and ran back to my house for help. My head was all junky." His words come between sloppy cries and tears. "When I opened the door again…I seen my poppa. I looked a fright all covered in blood, but I was trying to explain. I…I tried to tell him I needed help, but he said I was casted! I was casted out of his house and headed for hell!"

"Indeed, Jakabie…indeed."

"So, we drove away in that man's car."

"The whole time?" My mind attempts to digest how this moron could have evaded the authorities. *"The entire time?"*

"Yes, ma'am."

I stand. I'll never see my brother again and it's because of this piece of dung, nestled among shit. He took Carter from me and I can't seek revenge because the kid has the answers I need. It's then the realization sinks in. I grin.

"Wait…Jakabie. You're certain that man is dead? You know for sure?"

His body shakes as he cries. "Yes. I didn't mean to! I'm sorry!"

It's mine. It's *all* mine as soon as I get my hands on that little bitch and get her to that French-speaking cutie who threatened to slit me open…the entire payout will be mine! I can't control my cascading grin as excitement courses through me. "Oh. Oh, this is fucking scrumptious!"

The look on Jakabie's face is priceless as I turn to him. He's convinced I'm insane, but how many meek motherfuckers are running around pocketing seven digits? "Let's go, my little friend."

"Where?"

"To get Coty. We can't leave her alone. Can we?"

"Why do you want Coty, Ashlyn?" His tone is cold and solid.

"Duh, goofball. To take her back to her daddy."

"Why…why did your brother want her?" His pupils bounce in his sockets as his gaze traces my expression.

"No more questions." I lean forward, smiling happily. "We have a rescue mission and a reunion to oversee."

I nearly lose my breath as the sound of an approaching vehicle turns both our heads to the door.

"Shit." Before I can stand, truck doors are slamming and the voices of the boys who set me up here are heard outside. "Dammit. Keep quiet, my little hero." I grin sweetly. "I'll be right back."

Rushing, I meet the idiots on the porch.

"You catch 'em?" the larger guy, Justin, asks. They happily smile, peering up at me from the bottom of the steps.

"I wasn't expecting you this morning. Why are you back?"

Justin chuckles, slapping his bicep like an idiot. "I've got a can of whoop ass for that somebitch. Where is he?"

"Leave. Now. You're not supposed to be here." I glare at them, erasing their smiles.

Toby, the smaller one, weasels to the side of the house, looking through the window. "What's…what's going on in there?"

His eyes widen. He's seen my bound quarry.

"Holy…holy shit. Why…why is that…"

"Fuck." I walk past Justin to the truck, retrieving the keys from the ignition and their cellphones from the drink holders. I look to the porch to see Justin has made his way into the house while Toby stares through the window. A rusty screwdriver rests in the floorboard of the truck. It's perfect.

"Toby." I walk to him. "You don't understand. You could never understand." Taking his hesitant hand, I nudge him toward the bed of the truck. He half-sits on the tailgate.

"Why…what's going on? Is that…is that Jakabie Mathews? That missing kid? I know that guy."

His smooth baby-face cheek is feather-soft on my lips as I kiss his face. "This had to be done."

His eyes—it's all there in his pretty little eyes. He doesn't understand. He isn't toxic, but pure. "Did you call the police? Does he need an ambulance?"

"Sshhh, Toby."

His hands grip my shoulders for support as the entire shank disappears into his chest and into his heart. He stares at the handle, pulsating between his ribs, and then he looks at me, his eyes pleading as the light fades from them.

"That's a good boy, Toby. Just rest." I help him lie back as he fades in my arms. "Silly kid. Why did you come out here? Look at the mess you've made." I hoist myself in the bed, pulling Toby up in the truck as he dies.

"Justin."

Up the steps and in the home, I see my stocky friend. Justin is bent over, working diligently to free Jakabie.

"Your crack is showing," I announce gleefully.

He turns to me. "You never said anything about this! This is crazy!" He looks past me. "Toby!"

I grin. "He's waiting for you in the truck."

He ducks, glancing out the window to see Toby's feet dangling off the edge of the bed. "Toby?"

"Better hurry. You might catch his last words."

I squat to Jakabie, locking gazes with him as we hear Justin wail like a pantywaist outside over his dead little brother.

"What did you do?" Jakabie asks.

"I killed him." I chuckle.

"You! You're a bad person." His struggling stirs dust as I stand.

"Oh, well, that's not nice. Jakabie, if you don't take me to Coty, no one will ever find her and she'll die too…just like Toby…and just like your parents."

His struggles cease as he stares, wide-eyed at my smile. "What?"

"That's right, Jak. Momma and Poppa…they're dead. Both of them."

His head shakes rapidly. "No!"

"Yes!" I shout back.

"No, no, no!" Tears dot the dusty floor below him as he cries like a pitiful pussy.

I continue giggling as I make my way from the house to find Justin searching for his missing keys. "Missing something, buddy?"

"You bitch! You whore!" Stumbling toward me, wiping his eyes, he shakes his head. "Why? Why would you do that?"

"Oh. Boo fucking hoo. You came out here and took a big shit. Now I'm left to wipe it off my shoes. Am I crying about it? No. Shut the fuck up." I rush him, screwdriver in hand. I watch the shank sink halfway into his belly before my world goes dark.

I open my eyes to the sky above me and Justin's cries of pain. I realize I've been punched in the face and knocked on my ass. There's no time for further analysis.

On my feet, I locate the screwdriver and the cowardly Justin.

"Please!" He stumbles, landing on his knee as he cries out.

"Stop. None of that." Blood streams from my mouth and nose. "You know I have to kill you, Justin. There's really no other option."

"I don't…please, I don't wanna die!"

His cries for mercy won't spare his meaningless life, but I honestly do wish these boys would have just stayed home and played X-Box or jacked-off this morning. They're both sweet guys and killing them is more of an inconvenience than anything.

"I'll make you a deal," I say softly.

His whimpering stops long enough for him to focus. "You're a bit bigger than Toby…huh? Fried chicken…baby-fat?"

"What? Please don't kill me. I'm bleeding—"

"Don't interrupt me! Rude!" I step closer. "If you walk like a gentleman to the bed of the truck, I promise you this will be painless. But if you make me drag your butt across this yard, I'm going to hurt you, Justin."

"I'm…why are you doing this? I don't want to die."

"I know. I get it. But you have to. So, let's do this the easy way…and walk on over there."

He stands, grabbing his belly and wincing. "Can you help me? I'm—I can't walk too good. I feel woozy."

From one stab wound? *Weak!* "Of course, sweetheart."

The instant I'm within striking distance, I realize I've made an awful mistake. Justin is stocky, not chubby. He's built like a corn-fed farm boy with a bit of gym rat in him.

He played me, and now I'm on the ground, his face coming into view between blackness like a movie reel. His fists don't hurt, yet I know they're damaging as they come down on me and my hands are empty.

The beating halts as his trembling grasp works its way around my throat. There's a recognition…a connection to the rage and darkness in his eyes as he stares down at me. And then my desperate hand fumbles upon my lost weapon—the screwdriver. Justin yelps as I plunge it into his side. He releases me just in time to pull it out and stab him again.

I'm able to catch my breath when he jumps from me, but from the ground I watch him stagger across the yard and he's swallowed up in a cornfield.

"Dammit!" With no time to waste. I leap into his truck and tear from the yard in his direction. The truck slices into the crop yet there's no thud—no white trash caught under my tires.

I drive deep into the field before turning the truck off. "Justin! Come back, boy. Let's work something out. There's no need to run off."

Fuck this. I walk, battered and bleeding, back toward Jakabie.

If I never see another goddamned cornfield again…I step from the field and hobble to the house. No more fucking around. It's time to grab Jakabie and get the fuck away from this dump. Up the steps, and through the door, and what the fuck?

A shivering Jakabie is sitting, working to free his feet from the tape I secured him with. "You need help with that, sweetheart?"

"Get back!" He points a handgun at me…Carter's handgun. "I'm not stupid!" His gaze and aim are locked on my face.

"Oh. Well, kiddo…that's debatable. I'd say you're dumb as fuck, but that's just my opinion. Did you have that gun the entire time? You goof. I could have really used that thing about two minutes ago. Here's to looking out, Jak."

"I'm not stupid."

"Okay, you've stated that once already. Are you ready to go get Coty?"

"Did you kill my folks?" The way his gaze is locked on me…he's going to kill me if I mutter one misplaced word.

"No. No, Jakabie. I had nothing to do with that, I promise."

"Why did you kill them boys?" His voice cracks.

"Those boys were horrible, awful people—"

"No! Justin was good to me! At church, he was good to me. Toby, too!" He studies me, his hands are steady, as is his aim.

"Okay…well, you'll be happy to know that Justin was alive last I saw him."

My mouth and eyes are dry and dusty in the house's filth. This night has been exhausting and I don't have the patience for this shit any longer. "Jakabie, dammit, put the gun down. Now. Let me take the tape off of you so we can go save Coty. You know she's scared right now, right?"

"No."

"Jakabie. What are you going to do? Shoot me? No one is going to believe you. If you hurt me, the police are going to arrest you. They're going to touch you."

"I won't take you to Coty. I know what I did was wrong…I know it. But I won't let you hurt her."

I sigh. "Please put the gun down. No one is coming for you. No one is going to help you, and the only way you are going to get back to Coty is with me. Let's do this together. We can get her back to her daddy and we'll all be okay. You can trust me. I promise."

"No."

At this point, I'm ready to risk taking a bullet just to rush him and beat the fuck out of him. "Jakabie, you're seriously about to piss me the fuck off. What are your options? You can either let me get that nasty tape off of you so we can go get Coty…shoot me and go to prison with a whole bunch of nasty men just like Gary, or we stand here while you point a gun at me like a fucking idiot. Only one of those options sounds reasonable."

He shakes his head. "We're waiting."

"Waiting on what, dumbass?"

"You said Justin was alive…he'll get help."

I laugh. "You silly goose. We're at least a ten-minute drive from town and Justin has been stabbed three times with a screwdriver. He'll have bled out long before he makes it for help. Let's go—"

"He's going to call the police. I told him what you done to me and he's calling the police."

I smile gleefully. "No, silly. I have both his and his brother's phones." My arms cross as I shake my head.

"I gave him the phone from that man. He'll use it."

My heart races. "What? Carter's phone? You had

it?"

"Yes."

Uncrossing my arms, I step in his direction, only to have the gun follow me. "You won't shoot me, Jakabie."

"Yes, ma'am, I will."

He means it. My anxiety is peaking. "He…he doesn't have the password to Carter's phone, Jakabie. He can't unlock it."

"He don't need it to call nine-one-one. And it's got a full battery."

Five full seconds of dreadful silence have me wishing I'd have just tortured the information from him when I had the chance, or at least searched the fucker when he was unconscious. "Jak…Jakabie, please."

He only smirks. "Told you I wasn't stupid."

# Chapter Thirteen

### Drake

Black and burnt, the coffee leaves my tongue parched and does little to ward off the previous night's exhaustive exhibition. I'm clueless as to where Ashlyn might be. A sinking dread tells me her life is in danger, and given the circumstances, such a theory truly isn't that farfetched at all.

Coty and I would visit this tiny store frequently. We'd sit in this very booth while she enjoyed whatever treats she'd selected and I reviewed documents. Being here without her is odd. My life now is odd.

The police station isn't far from here. I could rush there and spill my thoughts at the risk of sounding crazy. Maybe I am crazy. Maybe Ashlyn is at some friend's house recovering from a bottle of wine and a girls' night in. Perhaps her phone was on silent because she legitimately needed a break from this psychosis I'm now calling reality.

"Hey, Doc." Bernadine Redland sits down across from me.

"Oh, hello there."

"We're praying for you at the Nazarene, Doc. The whole town is praying for you." Bernadine is kind. She's in her eighties, but moves about with ease and is highly social.

"I appreciate that, Bernie."

"You make sure to take care of yourself, okay? A man can't live without proper nutrition."

I only smile.

"Take care, Doc."

"You too, Bernie."

Bernie leaves, only to be replaced by Girtie. I typically tolerate Girtie's company. Her lack of hygiene and comical expressions have led to many colorful conversations between Coty and me.

"Howdy do, Drake Graves."

"Hi."

"You're lookin' about as beat up as the tail-end of a coonhound in heat."

"Um. Yeah. It was a long night last night."

Like roadkill, her smile is both hard to look at and hard to glance away from.

"I tell ya…it's dryin' up round here. We gotta get some business or this little ol' town is just gonna shrivel on up and blow away."

"Girtie…I'm sorry, but I'm just not in the mood for company right now."

She appears heartbroken. "Oh. Okay. You tell Coty I said hello."

Now I feel awful. For a town gossiper, she doesn't keep up with the latest trends.

"And…and tell your girly I hope she found't her brother."

"What?" I stand. "What did you just say?"

A stunned Girtie turns to me. "Ashlyn. Aren't you two sweet on each other? I thought you was an item. If not—"

"When was the last time you saw Ashlyn?"

"Yesterdee evening."

"Okay. Girtie, this is important. I can't find Ashlyn. Do you know where she was going?"

She smiles. "Sure enough do!"

Silence.

"Okay, then, Girtie. Do you think you could tell me where she was going?"

"Oh. Yes, sir. I told her about her brother Carter's vehicle being parked out on Six-Mile Road off at Gilly's demo site. I seen it there a few evenings when I was headin' home."

"She said she was going there?"

"Yes, sir. She flew out this lot like a rabid bat out of hell to get to him. I always did thought they was too close. But I guess family is family."

"Thank you, Girtie. You have an excellent day."

I jump in my truck and leave the store. Why would Carter be at Gilly's demo site? And if he's there…then who was at Ashlyn's house last night playing with the lights? Regardless, nothing explains why Ashlyn hasn't answered her phone the entire night.

I fly down the highway with a renewed sense of hope. It isn't long and I'm seeing the small house in the distance, next to the massive cornfield. Dirt and gravel fly as I tear down the backroad and my heart nearly explodes when Carter's car comes into view. If he's here, then where the fuck is Ashlyn? Maybe he can tell me.

Parking just behind his car, I retrieve the handgun from the glovebox and close the door softly as I glance about the decrepit scene. "Hello? Carter Ramirez…are you here?"

Slowly, I walk toward the steps of the home, reaching for the railing as the front door flies open.

I'm horrified to see my mangled girlfriend rush from inside and basically leap from the steps and into my arms.

"Drake!" I nearly collapse with her to my chest.

"Ashlyn! What…what the hell happened to you?"

"He's inside!" Her tears…seeing the fear in her eyes has my blood boiling.

"Who? You're okay, Ash. Who is inside? Carter?"

Her swollen eyes continue streaming tears. "No, Drake…Jakabie."

My heart feels as though it literally has stopped beating. "What? What did you just say?"

"Jakabie is inside, just in there. He has a gun, we have to kill him!"

I hear her but it isn't registering. "Ashlyn, go wait for me in my vehicle. Let me—"

"No! Look at me, Drake!" I find my anger growing in bounds as I look upon her battered face. How someone could hurt her like this is mind-numbing to me. "Look at me, Drake. I can't lose you! I love you too much. You're my world…my everything." I feel her hands atop me and my gun.

"Give me the gun. It has to be done before someone else is hurt."

I pull away. Her injuries have her reacting out of fear.

"Dr. Graves." A shaky beckoning has Ashlyn and I

looking toward the porch to a bruised Jakabie, holding a gun.

"You…" There's a ghost only ten feet from me. The same ghost who stole my daughter.

"Give me the gun, Drake." Ashlyn's frosty whisper enters my ear.

"Jakabie…" I move in front of Ashlyn. "Why? Why did you hurt my daughter? Why did you take her from me?"

"I'm so sorry, Dr. Graves. I'm sorry." Almost inaudible, his words leave him in near-whispers.

"Where's the body, Jakabie?"

He craters, dropping to his knees. "I can…I can take you. I can't tell you."

"Tell me!" I yell out.

"I don't know."

His wailing should only be drawing anger from me, yet part of me longs to sit with him calmly and talk through this.

"That big grain bin past the school…the one before that old restaurant." He pauses, looking to me with pleading eyes.

"Jakabie! Tell me!"

"That house out there somewhere. That scary one they dress up for Halloween sometimes."

"What? Oh my god. That's nearly twelve miles from here…how?"

The sound of a vehicle starting catches my attention. A horrified Ashlyn tears from the scene in her brother's car. "Ashlyn! Wait."

The cloud of dust carries her away, leaving only me and my daughter's nightmare…both holding guns.

"Dr. Graves, please…I'm scared."

"Scared? Jakabie…" I shrug. "What do you want from me? You've taken everything from me. What is it that you want?"

"Please!" he mutters. "To give it back. I wanna give her back."

We stand in silence, staring one another down. I don't hate him. I want to. I want to think I'd be capable of his misery but I'm not. It's time for this to be over.

"Okay." I nod defeatedly as tears spill over my eyelids.

The escalating sound of police sirens catches our attention. To my left I see tiny lights rampaging in our direction down the highway.

Jakabie's eyes bounce from the brigade and back to me. They engorge with horror. "They're coming here for me?"

"Yes, Jakabie."

"No! No, no, no!" Shuffling feet have him nearly tripping over himself. "They'll touch me! They'll touch me and then the men like Gary will touch me!"

His frantic cries have me moving toward him. "Look at me, Jakabie."

"They're gonna touch—"

"Look at me!" I snap. "Yes, they are going to touch you when you are arrested. But it doesn't have to hurt. They don't have to hurt you, okay?"

He walks briskly down the steps toward me. "Okay." He waits intently for instructions.

"Give me your gun, bud." I take it and set both weapons near my truck under the front tire as the sirens scream louder.

Jakabie looks wildly about the scene, his fingers in his mouth as he cries.

"Hey. Look at me. Focus on me."

"I'm scared," He cries out. This monster who took my baby from me is scared and I can't find it in me to turn from him and leave him to his terror.

"Jak…Jakabie…come here." I raise my arms to him and he readily accepts my embrace. This boy typically shits a brick if someone accidentally grazes him, and now he quivers in my arms. He's horrified.

"I'm sorry, Dr. Graves."

I inhale and look toward the sky. My hands are cradling the kid who stole my daughter and cut short her precious life—the kid who sentenced me to walk my remaining days in desolation. My tears dot his t-shirt as I exhale. "I forgive you, Jakabie Mathews. I forgive you."

Sirens blare as tires slide on dirt. I continue staring toward the sky as doors slam behind me.

"On the ground! Now!" The overzealous shouting sends him further into panic.

As one, I move to the ground with Jakabie, ensuring his legs and arms are down and extended in a non-threatening position.

The commotion is quick, but I never take my eyes off Jakabie. And then they cuff him. He doesn't fight them, but his wailing is pathetically gut-wrenching.

The sirens are cut, leaving only Jakabie's cries in my ears. And then, a welcome voice.

"Get that man up." Officer Salizar calls from her car. "Off the ground! Now!" She exits the vehicle, racing to me as I'm lifted. An additional sedan produces Alvarado. He too approaches.

"Is this necessary?" I point to Jakabie. "He'll go willingly."

"Where is Ramirez?" Alvarado demands, his gun in hand.

"Ashlyn? I don't know. She…she got upset and left. I don't know exactly what happened here last night."

"He's in there, you all! Find him, now!" Salizar screams as officers disappear into the cornfield.

"What the…hell?" I ask as I look around, bewildered.

"Drake!" Alvarado snaps. "When did Ashlyn leave? Where did she go?"

"Oh my god, like, five minutes before you got here. I don't know where she is!"

"She's gonna hurt Coty!" Jakabie's muffled cry from the ground turns our heads.

"What the hell did you just say, Jak?" I squat to him, staring into his peering eyes.

"I told her where Coty was. That Ashlyn lady…she's gonna go take her. I know she's gonna hurt her."

I stare for an entire three seconds while attempting to absorb his words. "Hurt? Jak…Jakabie…is Coty…is my daughter alive?"

He scowls, an intense look of confusion distorts his expression. "Yeah. Of course she's alive."

"Ahhh." I'm on my ass. As if I've just fallen face first on the dirt road, the breath is knocked from me. "Oh, my…oh, my god. Oh, my god."

"He's here!" Officers shout in the distance as someone is carried from the corn on a stretcher. "He's alive!"

"Justin!" Jakabie screams out.

"What the fuck is going on! Where is my daughter, Jakabie? Is she really alive? Why did you take her? Tell me now!"

"I'm sorry! I was…I was trying to save her…I got scared."

"Save her from who?" I ask.

He rolls on his side, looking to the three of us. "Ashlyn calls him Carter. Coty calls him the scarecrow."

# Chapter Fourteen

### Ashlyn

This is emotion. It isn't fear. I think this emotion is just beyond that. Being this close to achieving my dreams, yet knowing they could be yanked from me when they're just within reach is petrifying. And yet, I'm exhilarated to know my tenacity might actually push me past the finish line.

Briefly, I imagine what I'd say to Carter if I pulled this off. The pride in his eyes and his encouraging words, telling me to chase my dreams…but that shit's gone now. This is what I'm left with. The idea of collecting the entire payout sends any hint of sadness into the atmosphere like the dust Carter's little car is kicking up. *Fuck it all*. Momma will be proud when I show up successfully loaded.

"There we are." The rearview mirror catches my grin and anticipation as the farmhouse Jakabie mentioned comes into view. There are too many random variables bouncing around. I haven't a clue how the fuck Drake knew to come to the demolition site…and if Justin was able to call for help, the pigs will swarm me like I'm a maple-glazed donut.

There isn't time for *what if*. The instant that brat is in my grasp my world will make sense. It has to. I've worked too hard for this and I'll be damned if a bunch of ingrates will sideswipe me last second and snatch my prize.

Taken by time, this red brick home surrounded by trees has vines crawling up the brick to the roof. There are two smaller buildings, one of which is completely consumed in vegetation, and a large wooden barn.

The instant the wheels come to a stop, I leap from the car and desperately glance over the property. *Where would she be?*

I rush to the front door to find it's locked. Through tall weeds, while swatting swarming insects away, I make my way to the back of the home to find its sun-bleached door is locked as well. Window paint and plastic Halloween sheet signs hang in the windows, obstructing my view.

Kicking in the back door or breaking a window is an option, but first I'll take a quick glance in the barn. Neither Coty nor Jakabie are intelligent creatures, and I wouldn't put it past the idiots to sleep in a barn when there's a stable house sitting right next to it.

Hot, dry, and dusty, a mild breeze blows through the barn as I jog toward it. It carries with it something familiar…a scent. Much like the shoeboxes under Carter's childhood bed, this smell is distinctive and disgusting. I envision Coty's corpse, decaying in the August heat, and with it…my livelihood. The barn boasts multiple stalls, but my nostrils lead me right past the first four and to the darkest corner on the right.

Like the intro to some sadistic tune or film, the atmosphere around me is thick with the high pitched buzzing of countless flies. So overwhelming is the stench that I'm now breathing through my mouth…but the taste of death soaks into my tongue. This isn't a squirrel or a small puppy, tortured and tucked away to rot under my brother's bed…this is bigger.

Inching toward the wooden stall door, it groans as I open it…as if it's warning me to turn my gaze from what it's hiding. *I have to know.*

As the door swings in, the black curtain of flies opens widely as they ascend…allowing their work to come into view.

My hand slaps over my mouth. This is emotion…*but what is it?* Tiny maggots bead my brother's bloated face like stretching, crawling pearls. They fall clumsily from his cheeks and nostrils to the straw beneath him.

His eyes…they're not peering at me. The putrid little things have taken my brother's beautiful eyes and have left me to stare into their off-white swarm. They writhe and fatten on his rotting flesh within his sockets.

I gag, turning from Carter and eyeing the red brick through the barn opening. "I'll kill her."

No coaxing, no sweet words or gentle prodding. I'll rip her from her world the way she and that fucking nutcase took Carter from mine. I want to hurt her first. Before I give her away, I want her to cry before me and know that her life will forever be altered.

Charging from the barn, exhaling the last of my brother's death from my lungs, I run to the front door.

Dust, pieces of wood, and cracking noises fill the entryway as I slam through the doorway. What the fuck is the point of a beautiful, thick wooden door if it's secured by a pansy-ass locking device?

"Coty? Where are you?" I yell out, making my way into the musky smelling kitchen. The counter is littered with Gatorade bottles, candy wrappers, and chip bags. "Coty!"

Only silence as I tear across the worn linoleum and to the living room of the home. Two pallets of blankets lie on the floor. Boxes of Halloween decorations line the walls.

"That little brat," I mumble.

A door off the living room leads to a staircase. Peering down, the basement appears well lit from ground windows.

Plush, red carpet covers the steps as I descend. "Coty? Coty, are you down here?"

A scurrying from below halts my steps. "Coty?"

"Who…who's there?" her tiny voice calls back.

"Coty, it's Ashlyn. Come here, *right now!*" Tiny feet slap on the cement flooring as she runs to the stairs.

"Ashlyn…what's the matter with your face?" She steps back, apparently horrified by my appearance. She apparently doesn't have access to a mirror. If I didn't know better, I'd say this heathen just crawled from the bottom of fast food dumpster. Greasy little skank!

Charging down the stairs, I grab her arm, yanking her to me. "You! Coty! Do you have any idea what you have done? Do you know how much trouble you're in?"

Instantly with the waterworks. And this kid smells like a damn litter box. I'm so over this shit.

"Ashlyn…I want my dad. Where is Jakabie—"

"You will *never* see Jakabie again, you stupid little brat." I pull her frightened face closer. "And…you are going to be punished appropriately for what you and that fucking retard did to my brother. You will never, *ever* see your daddy again."

"No!"

"Yes!"

Her feet aren't able to maintain footing, so I'm basically dragging her up the stairs.

I emerge victorious as we step from the home and into the sunlight.

"Please! I want my daddy!"

In one second I'm on her level and in her face like a schoolyard bully at recess. "And *I* want my brother, but guess what? He's dead because of what you and your stupid friend did!"

"Please!" she cries. Snot and tears assure me that my next job will be a dead or alive option because I can't deal with these yuppie white fuckers who gasp every time someone gets a boo-boo or is killed.

"No. No, ma'am, Coty. You did the crime and you will be punished." I stand as she yanks backward from my grasp.

"I did nothing!"

"You little brat!" A handful of her nasty ass hair brings her face within inches of mine. "You did nothing? What about my brother? What about the man Jakabie hurt?"

"The scarecrow?" she whimpers.

I chuckle. "That's cute, Coty. Scarecrows don't…shut up."

"Ashlyn—"

"Shut the fuck up!" My eyes widen as I stand. It isn't my imagination. Sirens are calling over the fields around us. Little demons screeching out, letting me know they're coming to take my all…everything.

"Let's go! Now!"

"Ashlyn!"

"Now!" I toss her in the front seat as I jump in. "Put that seatbelt on now, Coty! I can't have my future flying through the windshield."

"I'm very scared—"

*"Nooowww!"* My belligerence brings me over the console, leaving her cowering and staring at me in disbelief as she reaches for the seatbelt.

"That's…that's right, Coty. It's best to mind."

Rather than tear from the farm, leaving a dusty visual, I creep away down the drive while formulating a plan. A right turn onto the dirt road leading to the farm and I'm grinning. "Yes. Oh yes. We have a shot."

The vibration from my pocket has me fishing my phone to see Blocked Caller. *Beautiful!*

"Hello? Sherri? I have her! I have her with me now! We did it!"

*"Stand down, Ashlyn."* Masculine and deep, the tone of the guy from my house fills my ear.

"What? Say what? I coming to you now, cutie-pie. I hope you've got room for one more because I need a bailout right about—"

*"Stand down, Ashlyn. The deal is off."*

Every muscle in my body relaxes as my smile fades. The car slows to a crawl. "What? What the fuck do you mean?"

*"Stand down. This has gotten out of control—"*

"No, motherfucker. You listen to me. I have this little witch with me right now. Either you take her or she's as good as dead!"

*"You listen to me, Ashlyn! If anything happens to the*

*granddaughter…I will find you."*

"No!" I look around. "What am I…what am I supposed to do?"

A cold chuckle enters my ear. *"Something else."* The bastard hangs up on me.

"Goddammit!" My foot meets the floorboard as dirt and rocks fly on either side of the vehicle and the car fishtails to full acceleration.

"This isn't happening. How is this happening? How?"

I'd been so concerned with watching for red and blues in the rearview that the barricade of officers coming into view just over the hill comes as a complete shock. Without a second thought, I veer to the right and soar from the road.

*"Ashlyn!"*

I see nothing but white…powdered white. Coty's shrieking and the dying engine flood my ears.

"No…" My own blood speckles the deflated airbag before me. I'm lost. All I have worked for is gone. Hot wind turns my attention to my right. I'm only now realizing the passenger door is open and that little heathen is gone. My payday has become my life insurance. I have to get her.

"Coty!" Out of the car, I look upon a field of tall, dead weeds. Even worse than corn. Sirens blare as I glance to the sky. Fuck it. Fuck it all.

I walk defeatedly toward the road, my head shaking and knowing there are only two ways this can go. Coty is nowhere in sight as I take a seat in the ditch and wait for my fate.

This is emotion. I'm pissed, and I'm confined, and there isn't a goddamned thing I can do about it but wait here. I have to sit here while these fuckers take it all away right in front of me. *Fuck that.*

I stand as the pig patrol pulls up and surrounds me from both sides of the road.

Several swine exit their vehicles, but that fat fuck Alvarado is the bastard I'm staring down. He jumps from his car as fast as his hefty self can manage and hobbles in my direction like he's figured something out.

"Get down!" he shouts. "Now!"

"Um. No. Go suck a shotgun, you fat fuck," I shout back. "You don't tell me what to do."

And then I see him. Drake's candy ass, crying, as usual, is at Salizar's side…her hoof to his chest to ensure he doesn't get too close. He stares at me in disbelief.

"What?" I look directly at him.

"Where is she? Where is Coty?"

I shrug. "I don't fucking know. The brat bailed as soon as the car died. She's out there, just waiting for the climactic reunion. Stupid brat."

His shaking head is nearly enough to evoke laughter, but I have at least a dozen hogs with handguns all pointed at me.

"How could you do this to me, Ash? I love…I loved you."

It's too much…seriously too much. "Do you fucking hear yourself right now? I'm standing here with these piss-ignorant assholes ready to let 'er rip, after I have literally lost *everything!* And you are going to stand there and ask me how I could do this to you? Are you even serious right now? Fuck you, Drake! I fucking hate your momma's boy ass! I hate you *so* much!"

"Get on the ground now!" Alvarado repeats.

"Or what? Shoot me!" I scream. "You're all insignificant. All soft and useless." I spit on the ground.

"Ashlyn," Drake whimpers, "the entire time?"

"Yes! You stupid fuck!"

"We know about you co-conspiring with your brother, Carter," Salizar says.

"Really? You *dumbass,* bull dike-looking bitch!" I laugh. "Your fine detective skills are on point…but they didn't quite get the job done in time, did they?" I nod, smiling. The fact that Drake looks as though he might pass out is possibly even better than the payday.

"We know you made the pond call," Alvarado interjects.

"Oh…that's a start," I say with a smile.

"We know you planted the sandwich crusts the same night at the clinic," he continues.

"That's some strong effort there, fat ass, but ya just missed the special, extra wide seat on the short bus. Ya didn't quite put it all together in time to save that drag queen-looking cunt, Ms. Gonzalez, did you? Or Toby…or Justin—"

"We saved Justin," Alvarado announces proudly. "He's going to make it."

"Oh! Well, isn't that precious. Guess who you didn't save?" I look directly at Drake. "Biggles…dear, sweet Biggles."

His gaze narrows on me, it's clear he's in shock.

"I hope like *fuck* you enjoyed your *chicken* enchiladas." I smile proudly as all pigmentation fades from his face.

"You sick bitch." Alvarado shakes his head.

"Ashlyn…you are certain Coty Graves is in this vicinity?" Alvarado demands as he moves closer.

"Yes, ugly. I'm done with this shit. Arrest me."

"Get on the ground, Ramirez," Salizar squeals.

"No. I will not." Vibration in my pocket has me envisioning that bitch, Sherri's face, as I reach for my phone."

"She's going for a weapon!" Alvarado shouts.

His gunshot has me looking about, dumbfounded…and then I find I can't inhale. I can't breathe. There's a fire in my chest and I'm looking toward a steady rush of red cascading from the wound. "You…you p…pig."

I collapse and am surrounded. This is emotion. I'm scared. *This is it…Ash.*

The last thing I want to see as I fade from this fucking disgusting shithole is his face…but here he is, staring down on me once again as I stare skyward. "Drake."

"Ashlyn…can you hear me?" There's rage—fire and rage in his eyes…just like the fire in my chest. "I hope like *fuck* you enjoyed that bullet."

I grin as his face fades into black and the commotion behind him. Atta boy…*finally found his balls.*

# Chapter Fifteen

### Drake

This is hate. This is what hate feels like, and only an hour ago I looked at this traitorous thing as if she were my soulmate. The same officers who held their guns on her now work feverishly to maintain her.

Like a frenzy of lions at a kill, the officers have crowded tightly around Ashlyn as I walk backward. My attention turns to a field of sinister-appearing plant life. If what that lying bitch said was true…Coty might be in here.

My heart bounds. Knowing I may actually hold my living Coty in my arms once more has me racing for the field. "Coty!" I'm joined by two officers.

Clinging to my clothing, the thick, dehydrated vegetation makes it difficult to move and impossible to see the earth beneath it.

"Coty! It's Daddy! Please, baby-girl…please tell me where you are!" Tears blur my vision. "Coty, please—"

"Daddy!" Her tiny voice calls to me from the right.

"Daddy!" The waist-high weeds all but swallow her, but as my gaze rests on a mess of tangled brown hair from several hundred feet away, I sprint in her direction. "Coty! I'm here!"

"Daddy!"

Piercing thorns and scratching twigs ensure me I'm not dreaming. I'm seconds away from the only thing on the earth that matters, and when I get that little girl in my arms again, I'm never letting her go.

"Daddy, I'm scared!"

"Coty!" There are no words to describe what surges through me as I sweep my daughter from the brush and into my arms…back from the dead. "Coty!" Shaking and pliable, the only thing keeping my knees from collapsing is knowing we haven't a soft place to fall.

"Daddy!"

I've heard the expression, 'I'm speechless,' and even used it before…but only now does it make sense. I can't speak but can only squeeze my daughter and kiss her dirty face repeatedly as we cry together. She's come back to me.

Gone is her signature scent. I'm holding a pungent, sweaty little angel with I'm sure more dirt and debris in her hair than I've ever washed from her collectively. Sticks and twigs are trapped in the mess like flies in a web, but she's never been more beautiful.

"Oh, my baby! My baby girl!"

The grinning officers help guide us through the brush to the road. My knees hit the ground with Coty still in my arms.

"Daddy! Jakabie! We gotta help Jakabie!" Coty shrieks.

I hold her out to further examine her. Stained and

torn, her pajamas are a complete loss. A few superficial scratches line her face, but at first glance, she appears okay. She's okay…alive and standing right in front of me.

"Oh, Coty." I could kiss her precious face for days.

Salizar rushes to us. "Graves! Graves, is she okay?"

I look at her, grinning through my tears. "Yes."

Panting, Salizar catches her breath as other officers gather around us. "Graves, we'll need to get her to the hospital—"

"No!" she shrieks.

"Coty, I'm not leaving you, sweetie. I'll be with you the entire time."

"Daddy…Ashlyn! Please, don't let her come back. She's the worstest, meanest, ever! She said I could never see you or Jakabie again. She said she would kill me."

Such horrendous words, saturated with hate. How could she? What did Ashlyn consist of that made her such a cunning, cold predator? What do I consist of that I couldn't recognize her predatory gaze? I know it will take years of therapy to undo what that monster did…but I can't help but be overjoyed with the idea that we have those years back.

"Coty, you will never see Ashlyn again. And I am so sorry that I brought her into our home."

It isn't until the ambulance arrives and Coty is examined and gowned and loaded with me by her side that it sinks and settles…this is now my reality. I'm no longer one of *those* parents.

My face aches from smiling, yet I grin the entire ride to the hospital, and I'm incapable of wiping my joy away.

In the emergency room, the gentle physicians and nurses examine Coty closely. She's so exhausted, she sleeps the duration of the exam.

With Salizar by my side, I prepare myself for the physician's findings. Her expression is difficult to read initially, and then she smiles. "Some fluids and rest and she'll be as good as new, physically. I'm recommending an excellent therapist. I hope you'll follow up immediately?"

"Dr. Fields?" Salizar interjects hesitantly. "Did you find any…"

"No. There are absolutely no signs of sexual abuse, neither acutely nor from previous exposure. It is my medical opinion that your daughter has not suffered trauma of that nature."

Her words are a symphony entering my ears. "Thank you. That's…that's beautiful." I kiss my sleeping daughter.

Alvarado listens from the doorway. He knocks gently before entering the room. "May I?" Producing a folder and handing it to Salizar, he shakes his head. "This is just unbelievable."

"How's Jak?" I ask curiously.

"He's sleeping." A heavy sigh leaves him. "I assumed he was just another sad story…continuing the cycle of abuse. This isn't that at all."

"I should have listened to my gut," I mutter.

"No." Salizar giggles. "I say you never listen to your gut again. I vote intense background checks and private investigations."

I chuckle. "It still hasn't sunk in, ya know? It's like…I hadn't had time for the shock of my daughter's death to fully absorb, and now she's right here. She's okay."

"You're okay," says Alvarado. "And you're going to be okay. One of the perks of our jobs is watching people and families overcome the adversity that's been thrown at them. You two are going to make it past this."

"That's right." Salizar brushes Coty's hair from her face.

"She's going to be horrified. Tonight, when we're back in that house—"

"Graves," Salizar interrupts. "You do what it takes. Let her cuddle up with you. And I'm approving an officer to sit at your house overnight. That might help?"

"I'm sure. It's completely unnecessary, but it'll help me, if anything—"

"Dr. Graves," Alvarado interrupts, "the reality is, the only thing we truly know about your daughter's case is two lowlifes conspired to abduct her. Until we iron out the facts completely, it's better to be safe."

"I agree," Salizar confirms.

"And Jakabie. When will he be able to leave?"

Salizar stretches as she stands. "The District Attorney is reviewing evidence as we speak. I'm certain he'll be free to leave custody by week's end. There's an excellent home for—"

"A home? What do you mean, a home?"

"Drake." She cocks her head. "Jakabie Mathews can't go home to his parents' house. He needs to be in a place—"

"Jak will be fine. He's not going to a group home."

"Drake, Jakabie—"

"The only thing I can say with absolute certainty is that if not for Jakabie Mathews, my daughter wouldn't be sleeping in front of me right now. Some of the first words out of Coty's mouth when I pulled her from those weeds were regarding that kid's well-being. She loves him. So do I."

Salizar returns to her seat, looking to me. "Okay, that doesn't change the fact that he needs—"

"Right now, he needs family. Coty and I are family. There are three empty bedrooms in my house for that boy to choose from. He's not going to a home. Tell your D.A. friend that."

# Chapter Sixteen

Bubbles, LOL dolls, Barbie dolls, and chin-level water have Coty grinning mildly. Fresh-faced with sudsy hair, this little human is doing what little humans do…but I know she's churning inside with questions that might not come to the surface for days or even years.

Each time our gazes meet, I can't help but smile. Pure torture was the idea that my daughter was decaying in a cesspool of excrement. Also excruciating was not knowing of the events leading up to that…just this morning I was ignorant of so much and left to assume the absolute worst.

"Coty…tell me, did Jakabie give you a picture?"

Bubbles part as tiny, pruned fingers trace along the top of the water. "Lots."

"Lots? He gave you lots of pictures?"

"Yeah." She smiles. "We drawed pictures. We always do."

"And, the pictures…some of them are sad? Do you draw sad pictures?"

Little bubbles slide from her fingers in front of her

face. "Nope."

"Oh. Coty…I saw a sad picture. Do you know about that? There was a really sad picture in your bedroom."

She nods. "Yeah. Jakabie gave'd it to me."

"Okay. Can you tell me why he gave it to you?"

"I'm not supposed to say. It's our secret." She reaches for her floating doll.

"Coty, we shouldn't keep secrets. This is important. Can you please tell me why he gave you that picture?"

"Daaaaddy."

"Please, Coty."

"Jakabie's voice used to didn't work when he was little. But no one can ever make me to be quiet. Jakabie says so."

"Coty, who is in that picture?"

"It's Jakabie when he was just little like me, and a bad guy. Jakabie says no one can touch my body because its mine…my own. He says if someone touches me like that, they're in big trouble."

"Coty…has anyone ever? Has anybody ever touched you like in that picture?"

She frowns. "No. Not me. Daddy, that's why he's sad. That's why he cries."

"Who?"

"Jakabie. He got hurted when he was little." Tiny tears fall from her chin to the water below her.

"Listen to me, Coty. We are going to do everything possible to help him. Okay?"

"We have to, Daddy. He saved me. He took me from the scarecrow."

Dried and dressed, I hold my sleepy daughter in my arms. Twelve hours ago, I was living and breathing without my heart, and now it's back and overflowing with joy.

"Daddy," she speaks and yawns at the same time.

"Yes, baby-doll."

"Who is Sherri?"

"What? Why would you ask that, Coty?"

"Ashlyn…meany Ashlyn was yelling at her on the phone."

"What? Coty…" Her eyelids flutter, she's out. The comment makes no sense. Even if Ashlyn was yelling at a Sherri, it is certainly some scum she's associated with and not Coty's estranged grandmother.

Soft knocks on the front door coax me through the kitchen, Coty in my arms. My house is a home again. My life is whole. The mental fortitude needed to dissect and digest the circumstances surrounding my lovely ex-girlfriend and our farce of a relationship will be staggering, but I'm surprisingly unconcerned with that at this point.

Opening the door, I'm surprised to see Special Agent Alvarado. "Hey there," I whisper.

"Graves."

"Is…is everything okay?"

"Perfect. I'm all yours tonight." He grins. "May I?"

I step aside, allowing him to enter. "You? They hooked us up."

"I'm off the clock, Graves. I figured, what the hell? Rather than burn a rookie, I'd just come out and have a beer…share some intel, and crash on the couch?"

"Sounds great, man. There's some cold ones in the fridge."

In the living room, Coty wrapped like a caterpillar—snoozing with her head in my lap, Alvarado and I share a few laughs and a few beers. Knowing the conversation will take a darker, more serious turn soon allows the alcohol to cascade freely down my throat.

"Have you always done abductions?"

He swallows the last of his bottle. "No. No, actually I started in sex-trafficking. I was part of a task force in Vermont. We brought a lot of girls, and guys, home. Put a lot of bad ones behind bars."

"How'd you end up here?"

He chuckles. "I got a phone call. Pretty little girl went missing and my expertise in the field was needed."

"You're only here for Coty?" I ask appreciatively.

"Mainly. I'm heading the field forensics and overseeing the analyzation of all the case specifics until we clear some details."

"Everything's happened so fast. I haven't had time to ask why. Why did this happen? What did they want? Ashlyn has been a part of my life for a year now. If it was all for *this*…then what is it? What were they wanting?"

"Money. They wanted your money, Graves. When your parents passed away, you were left with a trust fund, yes?"

"Yeah." The pieces begin connecting.

"These vultures knew that. I've dismembered Ashlyn and Carter's profiles. They come from tainted bloodlines. This was done out of a pure, evil, and selfish lust for cash."

"Why? Why not just take her? Why wait an entire year—"

"Their phones were recovered. I'm personally overseeing the data recovery from those devices. I'm assuming we'll know more once that occurs."

"How? How could I have been so blind? Look at how many people were hurt because of them. And I spent my nights cursing Jakabie and imagining doing awful things to him…when he was Coty's hero."

Alvarado stands. "Drake…there are going to be plenty of opportunities for you to wonder why, and beat yourself up for this and that. Make sure you're giving yourself credit where it's due. You were dealing with two cold-hearted sociopaths, hellbent on getting what they wanted from you. That's on them, not you. Ashlyn Ramirez was just good at what she was doing."

I nod.

"I've got to take this. Beer?" he asks, holding his phone up as he walks backward to the kitchen.

"Yeah. I'll take one more."

There's nothing I want more than to push Ashlyn from my memory. The joy of having Coty back and breathing hasn't allowed me the opportunity to truly absorb the atrociousness of the situation. I loved her, and she did *this* for money.

My thirst has me walking to the kitchen when Alvarado doesn't return immediately. I peer back at my daughter as I do. Alvarado is on the porch, speaking with someone over the phone.

Two beers in hand, I step to the screen door.

*"Ca se passe ce soir,"* I hear him say softly. His head reflects the glowing, dim light of the porch. *"Je vais m'en occuper…juste etre la."*

Bewildered, I scuffle back to the living room, sitting next to Coty.

Seconds later, Alvarado enters. "Oh…you grabbed some cold ones already, I see. I'll put these back." He holds up two beers.

"I didn't know you speak French."

He forces a smile. "Yes. Yeah, I was born and raised in Montreal. My momma is French-Canadian."

"Oh. I assumed…your name."

"No worries, my man! My daddy was from Panama. I'm a strange breed, but I think we all are when you break us down and see what's inside."

"Yes. Yes, that's true."

"I'll just be right back, Graves," he says.

The floors groan even louder than usual when Alvarado traipses across them. He sits across from me.

"So, what exactly is happening tonight, Alvarado?"

"Excuse me?" Head cocked, he appears dumbfounded.

"On the phone…I wasn't trying to eavesdrop, but I couldn't help but overhear your conversation."

He nods. "I was wishing my mother a happy birthday. Today's her birthday."

"Oh…how old?"

"Um. She's getting up there." He chuckles.

"Yeah, it's just you said…*it's happening tonight*…and you told your *mother* that you would *take care of it*. And that to *just be there*."

His smile fades. "*Tu parle Francais?*"

"Clearly." I lean forward. "You can imagine, after everything that's happened, why I might be paranoid?"

"Certainly." He grins.

Salizar's name appears on my screen as my phone vibrates atop the coffee table.

"Nope," Alvarado says as I reach for it.

"What…what's going on?"

Alvarado removes his gun from the holster as he stands. "You wouldn't understand. There's really no point in explaining."

"What? No. Please, tell me what this is. What are you doing here?"

"Graves, buddy. You have been through quite the ordeal. Let me…shed a little light. I haven't been truthful with you, bud."

"You're scaring me, Alvarado." I calmly collect my daughter from the cushions, shielding her in my lap.

"Don't be scared, man. That's not what I'm here for."

"Then why are you here?"

"I volunteered for this job, Graves…I wasn't recruited from Vermont. This wasn't supposed to happen like this."

"What? Look, dude, my brain can't take any more mindfucking. What is going on?"

"I'm finishing it."

"Finishing what?"

"I am finishing the job those two scumbags couldn't pull off. That's why I'm here. That's why I've been here."

"What?" I'm surrounded by snakes. The world is a pit of vipers, only many of them disguise themselves as friends and lovers rather than let their scales show.

"She'll be well taken care of, Drake. You don't have to worry about her wanting for anything."

My chest deflates.

"Hey…don't look at me like that. I'm not some psycho…I'm a man with needs."

"Why do you want my daughter?"

"I don't…her grandparents do."

"What! What the fuck did you just say to me?"

"Simmer down, bud." His free hand motions me to

calm.

"Don't you fucking tell me to simmer. Do you not hear what you're saying? Does it not sound ridiculous coming out of your mouth?"

"To you, I'm sure it does." He stands. "Please, allow me to tell you how this is going to take place."

"No. The audacity. You need to leave. Get the hell out of my house…now." Coty is deadweight in my arms as I stand.

"Soon enough."

"No. Now. You honestly think you can take her from my arms after she just came home to me? You're crazy."

His eyes follow me as he moves in my direction. I make my way through the house and to the kitchen. My keys are nowhere to be found, but my truck keys are always in the ignition. I glance at the exit, but he steps in between me and the door.

"Drake, I told you. Tonight will go specifically as I say. I'm not one for theatrics and all of that bullshit."

"Alvarado…why are you doing this? You know what I've been through. You know what Coty has been through."

He nods. "I understand. What I need you to understand is that this has been my intention the entire time. I'm not…"

Headlights and a car door closing silence him.

Heavy boots on the porch announce another party member as Salizar flings the screen door open—her weapon drawn.

"Well, well." Alvarado's menacing tone is greeted with a devious grin as Salizar enters the home. "Salizar. If it isn't my partner in crime."

She chuckles. "Fuck you. You're not my partner. You disgust me." Her gun is aimed intently at his head.

"What is it you think you know, Salizar?" he demands.

"Everything, you, asshole. I know you logged the phones from evidence…I know you've been in and out of Ashlyn Ramirez' home without a warrant. I know why you shot Ramirez…and most importantly, I know you're on Sherri and Dane Devereux's payroll."

Her reply seems to wipe the cocky smile from his face. "Busy little bee, Salizar…I underestimated you."

"Sure did."

"And yet, you show up without backup to arrest me? Not the smartest move…something a rookie would do…or a washed up cunt of a cop with baby issues."

She shakes her head. "You're not going to jail, Alvarado."

"What?" He grins. "You want in? I'll give you a decent cut if you can keep your fucking mouth shut."

"Shut up, Alvarado. Drake. Take Coty upstairs. Now." Salizar's command is stern and solid.

I don't argue. While shielding my daughter, I slip from the kitchen and race for the stairs. Nearly halfway up, a gunshot resounds through my home. Coty screams in my ear as we rush through her bedroom door, slamming it behind us.

"Daddy! What was that?" Her tiny arms squeeze tightly around my neck.

"Nothing, baby girl. You're fine. We're okay."

The stairs groan as someone ascends slowly. Cody remains in my arms as we back into the shadows of the corner of her bedroom. Seconds later, a tapping knock has me ready to fight to my last breath to ensure my daughter remains out of the hands of that bastard.

A river of relief washes over me as a reserved-looking Salizar enters.

"Holy shit. Oh my god, are you okay?" I ask her.

She enters, smiling. "Oh yeah. I am. Him…not so much."

"Thank you. Thank you so much. I had no idea. How did you know?"

She shakes her head. "I had a hunch. He was good, but he wasn't that good." She sweeps Coty's hair from her eyes.

"What are we going to do? Where will we go?"

"Once again, this place is an official crime scene. We'll get you set up. There's a bit of a mess in the kitchen."

"I can only imagine." I look to the ceiling, covered in My Little Pony and Barbie doll stickers. "I'm thirty years old and I'm going to have trust issues the rest of my life."

"Hey…I told you I would." She grins proudly.

"Told me you would what?"

She leans in closer to whisper, "I told you I'd shoot that motherfucker."

# Chapter Seventeen

My mother once told me, things that make no sense are either worth studying or worth nothing. Their actions made no sense.

Coty sits with her legs crossed. Her new kitten plays under her watchful eye—batting dandelions and falling clumsily. Gray and fluffy, the tiny addition to our family came as a gift from the eccentric Ms. Lewis. It's been nearly eight weeks since that morning…the morning Ashlyn Ramirez called my phone and forever changed my outlook on humanity.

My mind has to work to decipher it all some mornings. As if the past and present vomited in a bag and shook it around violently…leaving what's inside for me to pick through. Like sipping iced tea with Coty on my lap in the evening, and I'll hear a vehicle in the distance. Briefly, I'll smile inside as the idea of Ashlyn comes into my head. Then I remember I hate her more than the plague and my smile transforms into something sour…something nauseating.

The now, the present is something different. To glance at our home and yard, one might see nothing more than a loving father and happy daughter enjoying an October afternoon. I see the world through the eyes of a man who lost the most precious gift imaginable. Yes, I have her back, but the damage remains. Every bump in the night may originate from something sinister. Every stranger may be *that* stranger. *Normal* will forever be a word I smirk at.

Salizar's findings eviscerated my former in-laws' plans. Money may buy multiple homes and employ even the cruelest of the heartless, but kidnapping is frowned upon, regardless of who you are or your geographic location. Sherri and Dane were ultimately arrested. Their final plot to leave it all for alternative identities in Romania, where Dane had business ties, was crushed and discarded.

Initially, I believed the Devereauxs to be socially awkward and attributed that to their absence from Coty's life. The investigation proved most revealing in several aspects. Sherri and Dane are criminals to the core. Their livelihood and all they are is engrained with devious dealings, and learning this helps to piece things together in hindsight.

Coty will likely grow into adulthood without her mother, and certainly without her grandparents. I can only hope that when she's old enough to understand the truth, she respects me.

Besides me, with my inability to establish a healthy, romantic relationship with a healthy adult, I've concluded Renee and Ashlyn have something else in common...ingredients.

Some ingredients leave little option for a decent outcome...for example, enchiladas made of cat. Ashlyn Ramirez is wired wrong in the best way. Rather than mend, her mother taught Ashlyn to craft emotional wounds into weaponry for future utilization. The ingredients were spoiled from a young age. Her mother cultivated a cunning, cold-hearted predator. Predators have but one mission…to hunt. Her mission would have undoubtedly been successful had it not been for our friend, Jakabie.

Most of what comes from Jakabie's mouth is correct if a person will simply take the time to investigate his processing. I'll go through life acquiring regrets, as most people do, but one regret that will remain ulcerative on my soul is the fact that I allowed Ashlyn's twistedness to twist me up enough to hate that boy.

Dust and details have settled. A cruel light has been pointed directly at each of our wounds. Jakabie's wounds are old and deep, but at last, he's been given the intervention needed to mend.

"How much longer, Daddy?" She plucks white flowers from the lawn, placing them in her kitten's hair.

"Soon, Coty. We've waited this long."

"I'm bored, Daddy."

"So, play a game."

"Can we play I Spy?"

I shiver. "No. Anything but that."

The breeze brings with it a sense of renewal. Cool, with a hint of autumn, the season change is welcome and reminds me of home. A warm fire and spiced cider are on the menu for this evening. Much change has occurred, and yet, the thought of this colossal revolution on the brink of blooming has me grinning involuntarily.

A green Prius toddles toward our home like a pea with wheels. It isn't the clown-like car evoking my enthusiasm; rather, it's the cargo it carries.

In the past, I've told Jakabie I considered him family. Now's my time to prove that to him. It's not because I owe him for what he's done for me and Coty, but because I genuinely love the kid. Hell, I owe it to the world. If the most beautiful bird is never taught to fly, who will see its colors?

His ingredients are there…and they're great ingredients. He simply needs love, support, and family to ensure a fantastic outcome. We have an abundance of all three here.

"Coty. You see that?"

Pepper, the kitten, hisses and jumps inches upward as Coty screeches and jumps to her feet.

"Silly-head. You're going to give Pepper a nervous breakdown."

Kitten in arms, Coty runs to the side of the driveway. I'm soon at her side as we wait patiently for the car to come to a stop.

Salizar and Jakabie emerge. "I brought you something," she happily announces.

"We'll take him. Love your personal ride, by the way."

"Doing my part," she mumbles as she approaches. "You're sure about this?"

"How many times are you going to ask me that?"

"Okay. Well, it's official then." She pats my back. "And a…just so you know, it's over tomorrow. She's going in."

I shrug. "Who?"

We were able to visit Jakabie twice at the treatment facility. He totes a duffle bag of all his worldly possessions, a mile-wide smile, and infinite possibility.

"Hey, bud. How are you?" I cautiously extend a hand for him to shake—knowing full-well the offer may be disregarded.

"I'm well." Setting his bag down, Jakabie wraps his arms around me, hugging me.

"Oh." I'm instantly taken aback by the welcome change.

"Thank you, Dr. Graves," he says softly as he pulls away.

Coty clings to Jakabie's leg with Pepper in her other arm as I grab his bag and motion for the door. "Supper's not going to eat itself, you guys. Welcome home, bud."

# Chapter Eighteen

## Ashlyn

This is emotion. I know it's not fear. Fuck fear, that shit got me scarred and cuffed to this awful bed in this wretched-ass hospital. Perhaps it's an excitement of some sort? I'm convinced some emotions are best left unclassified. There are plenty of identifiable emotions. Each time a dumbass nurse or tech or respiratory therapist peeks their face into my room…anger. I'm over the lack of privacy. I get it. Ashlyn is horrible. Bad girl, Ashlyn! But seriously. Cuffing me to this nasty ass bed with a third-world style kettle to piss in is a bit ridiculous.

Another emotion is optimism. One might assume a person in my position has little to be optimistic about. Weeks ago, I thought the same.

It's amazing what a woman can learn to do with one hand alone.

Dr. Pedrina is complicated. His kind of complication doesn't come in layers. There's no onion there.

I wasn't trying. I'd all but accepted my future

destiny—to be fist-fucked repeatedly by Bertha in the penitentiary. Then he came…multiple times.

Cameron Pedrina, with a swoon-worthy face and a personality that could rival the awkwardness of first-time anal intercourse, entered my room to discuss my chest tube and the healing progression of my collapsed lung. My hospitalist in shining armor.

Visits became more frequent, conversations more casual. An order was written for a bedside commode and, ta da! His fingers massage where the catheter once was.

It's in his eyes…his tone, and the way he touches me when the door closes behind him. He wants every piece of me. He salivates and erects at the very sight of me…chained and disgusting while awaiting my fate.

The oddness lies in the fact that I wasn't trying. Cameron has full access to my file, my life, from their perspective, in words. He knows why I'm here, and still…his fingers find their way inside me each time the door closes.

As romantic as hospital-gowned orgasms may sound, all of that is superficial now. Dr. Pedrina's time at this level-one trauma center in Oklahoma City is ending. The thirty-two-year-old cutie is to return home to Mexico City to practice, a convenience whispered in my ear only weeks ago as my legs shook beneath him.

I might muster something like a longing for him tomorrow when I'm shackled and tossed into atrocious orange attire…if this doesn't work.

The fat, farting guard sits just outside my room. A monstrosity resembling Jabba the Hutt from *Star Wars*, the obese bastard does nothing but sit, nap, and watch Netflix. The biggest threat he poses is his ability to squeal and announce his findings, should he notice my absence.

The plan is simple enough. The difficulty lies in the execution and timing. I have absolutely nothing to lose and so much to gain. Cameron Pedrina stands to waste his world if this falls through. The man must have gotten a taste of something he loves.

"Ms. Ramirez?" His eyes bulge. Beads of sweat dot his forehead. As if he's just murdered a nun, Cameron's guilty expression is borderline comical as he approaches my bed, handing me a small key.

"Relax, silly fucker." My hand massages his crotch, cupping his balls at the bedside and tracing along his shaft until I feel the tension working its way from him and collecting in the swelling hard-on under his khakis. "Hey. When I get there…when we're both there, every night I'm with you I'm draining these fucking balls. You're going to ache." That's the thing with Cameron Pedrina. I've only been myself. There's been no deceit, no lies, and no cover-up. He knows what he's getting, and still, he comes back for more…licking his fingers as he leaves the room.

"That'll do, Ms. Ramirez." He grins. "He's out," he says, his voice low. "Scrubs and mask are in the bathroom. First floor. Take the skywalk to the top level of the parking garage, just outside the door. Gold Mercedes three-hundred. Keys and cash are in the glovebox."

"Okay. I'll see you in a few days." The cuffs slide off as I slip from the bed, watching him leave the room. It's an odd thing, telling the truth. If I'm not captured or killed, and my mother's connection collects me at the border in twelve hours, I mean it when I say I'll see him again.

It's eight in the evening now. Shift change. I position my pillows to resemble a sleeping Ashlyn in bed, change into the scrubs Cameron provided, and place the surgical mask on my face.

Cameron has written strict, do not disturb at night, orders for his bitch nurses. With luck, I'll be deep into Texas and Dr. Pedrina will be in the air by the time they notice I'm gone.

My heart races as I peer into the dark hallway to find Jabba sleeping soundly, his fat head resting on the wall behind him. The chattering nurses pay little attention to me on the elevator ride to the first floor. My gaze remains to the tile as I walk through the skywalk and toward my chariot…my luxury vehicle with cash, clothes, and a wig for disguise.

I'm still anticipating something to jump out at me…to fire at me or snatch me up like some monster as I pull away from the parking garage…but it doesn't. And it doesn't as I leave Oklahoma City. Hours later, the Entering Texas sign appears, and still…I'm anticipating *something*. Bad girls don't get happy endings. The bullet scar on my chest is proof of that.

It isn't until the dawn kisses my face, the car door slams, and that hideous blonde wig hits the sand that I realize I might have a shot.

"Ashlyn?" *Cual es tu nombre?* he asks. "Ashlyn Ramirez?"

We stand in desolation in front of the parked vehicle.

"Si." Hands held up submissively, I watch him—completely expecting him to produce a badge or gun.

"*Vamonos.*" He smiles. "*Tu madre esta esperando.*"

From prisoner to poverty, but I'm loving it. I climb into his shabby truck, my hands still shaking. This is emotion. I'm happy. I'll be meeting my mother soon, and the two of us will be bound for Mexico City to sit poolside and sip drinks and remember the good days. How is this my life right now? How was it this easy?

We pass playing children and I briefly think of Drake and wonder what his life consists of now. Occasionally I'll reminisce on our time together. There are times I wonder if pieces of what we had were real. Then I'm floored by his reactions to my situation toward the end of the debacle and I'm certain there's no way any of it was legitimate. That day…his cruel gaze and a dozen pistols aimed at me. No compassion as my world cratered. Fuck him. But then, fuck it. I'll be the bigger person. Perhaps I always have been. If a bad girl can have her happy ending, parrots, and palm trees, and a cute, awkward boyfriend who would leverage his entire existence for her, then I guess a selfish asshole like Drake and his wretched rug-rat should be awarded the same opportunity. I smile as my mother's face comes into view.

This is emotion…this is happiness. And I'm thinking there's more of it to come.


The End

# Acknowledgements

If you're reading this, thank you!

I have to give a huge shout out to my friend Carissa Ann Lynch for always being supportive of my work and giving me honest feedback.

As always, thank you to my beautiful wife and children.

# About the Author

Bradon Nave was born and raised in rural Oklahoma. He attended a small country school during junior high and high school, and graduated with only three people in his class. After graduate school, he decided to devote his spare time to his passion of writing. Bradon currently lives in Piedmont, Oklahoma, with his wife and two young children.

When he's not writing, he loves running, being with friends and family, and being outdoors.

**Facebook:**
http://www.facebook.com/bradonnavebooks

**Twitter:**
http://www.twitter.com/BradonNave

**Website:**
http://www.bradonnave.com/